THE MAGIC MEADOW

Westminster Press Books by
ALEXANDER KEY

The Magic Meadow

The Preposterous Adventures
of Swimmer

The Strange White Doves

Flight to the Lonesome Place

The Incredible Tide

The Golden Enemy

Escape to Witch Mountain

Mystery of the Sassafras Chair

The Forgotten Door

Rivets and Sprockets

THE
MAGIC
MEADOW

by
ALEXANDER KEY

THE WESTMINSTER PRESS
Philadelphia

Book design by Dorothy Alden Smith

Published by The Westminster Press₍ᵣ₎
Philadelphia, Pennsylvania

PRINTED IN THE UNITED STATES OF AMERICA

Library of Congress Cataloging in Publication Data

Key, Alexander, 1904–
  The magic meadow.

  SUMMARY: As five crippled children play games of imagining
themselves in another beautiful world, one of the boys finds he can
help the rest of them escape to a strange new place.
  [1. Science fiction] I. Title.
PZ7.K51Mag.   [Fic]   74–19194
ISBN 0–664–32561–0

This book,
in which something most extraordinary happens,
is about Brick and Diz Dobie and Lily Rose,
and Charlie Pill and Princess—
and it is dedicated to all of you
who understand them
and feel as they did,
and have come to believe that
practically anything is possible.

CONTENTS

THE MAGIC MEADOW

1

THE DANDELIONS

For a few startled seconds after he opened his eyes, Brick didn't know what to think. He couldn't quite believe what he saw, yet he was sure he wasn't dreaming. A few seconds ago it had been nearly midnight, and he had been lying in his bed in Ward Nine at Belleview, trying almost desperately to imagine the exact kind of place where he found himself now. Then a curious sound had made him turn his head and look about—and it seemed that the impossible had happened.

Belleview had vanished. Instead of the gloom and the dark, there was now a wonderfully warm sun cutting through the mist. Instead of on a hospital bed, he was lying on thick green grass, and there were clusters of bright-yellow flowers growing about him. The rumble of city traffic had ceased. In its place he could hear the singing of birds and the musical chatter of a tiny stream running past him down the hillside. As he listened, he was aware again of the curious sound that had made him open his eyes. He couldn't identify it, but somehow it didn't seem dangerous.

Brick hardly dared move. Was this real, or had it all been created by imagination? Not just his own, but the combined imaginations of all five of them back in Ward Nine?

Whether it was real or imaginary, something very strange had happened, and he had to find out all he could about it. . . .

*   *   *

They, the incurables, had been playing the "traveling" game a long time in Ward Nine. Every night, as soon as the lights were out and the hateful old building had quieted, they would close their eyes and begin to imagine where they would rather be instead of where they were. They had become pretty good at it—Brick, Charlie Pill, and Diz Dobie on the boys' side, and Princess and Lily Rose over in the girls' section beyond the big sliding screen.

They had persuaded Miss Jackson, the night nurse—who was a lot more understanding than the day nurses—to leave the screen partly open at night so that it would be easier to whisper together. Not that they really needed it open, for they had long ago figured out a way to talk secretly. But none of them had folks—no one in Belleview did—and they felt ever so much better and closer when they were not shut apart. After all, the only family that any of them had were the other four.

Princess was better at the traveling game than were the others. She had at least forty times their imagination. Give her half a minute, and she'd have you drifting down a Martian canal in a glass gondola, or maybe riding spotted dolphins through a coral forest, and all the while she'd be exclaiming and chattering away, almost making you believe the things she was pretending to see.

And then one night she'd surprised him by saying, "Brick, I like the place you tell us about better than any of the rest. It's so—so *real!* Do you s'pose there *is* such a place?"

"There must be," he told her. "If there wasn't, then how could we see it so clearly when we think about it?"

"Rats!" said Charlie Pill, who always saw the dark side of everything. "We've just been making it up for so long that we've sort of got to thinking of it as real."

"It's real to me," Lily Rose said wistfully. "And I sure wish we could be there."

They all agreed they'd rather be there than in a purely imaginative place like a castle on a cliff or a coral kingdom, or a red marble city on Mars. But Charlie Pill was doubtful.

"Okay," he said. "S'pose it's real, and say we're there. So what? It's just a hill with grass on it—"

"And *flowers*," Princess interrupted. "Don't ever forget the flowers. Wouldn't it be wonderful to see flowers growing on a hill?"

"Yes," Lily Rose whispered. "I've never seen a hill. Or flowers growing anywhere, except in a pot."

"Me neither," mumbled Diz Dobie, who seldom spoke. He was darker than Lily Rose, and might have been part Mexican or Indian. Lily Rose was more golden, while Princess was as pale as pale could be. Even her hair was silky white.

"Phooey," said Charlie Pill. "What good would it do us if we actually found ourselves in a place like that? I mean, heck, we couldn't run and play. We'd just have to lie there, and—and who'd look after us and feed us?"

Princess laughed. It was like the tinkling of a little silver bell. "Who cares? Why, if I could close my eyes and wake up on a hill with flowers, I wouldn't care about a thing in the world. I'd be so happy I'd be willing to die right there."

They were all silent a moment. Suddenly she said, "Brick, I've read that people can do anything if they really believe they can and—and try hard enough. If we all tried real hard, together, do you s'pose we could turn that hill into a real one, and—and sort of take ourselves there?"

"Why not?" he said. "It's sure worth giving it a whirl."

So they tried it that night and the next. Nothing happened except that the flowered hillside became a little more real and closer in their minds. Brick was ready for anything on the third night, but Charlie Pill spoiled it all by giving up early and saying the whole thing was silly.

Long after the others had stopped, more from weariness than from discouragement, and dropped off to sleep, Brick had kept doggedly at it. He'd been told more than once that red-headed people are stubborn; if so, it sure was a help, for he wasn't about to call it quits with that sunny hillside becoming ever brighter in his mind—so bright that he could actually feel the sun beating down on his face.

Then came that incredible moment when the curious noise caused him to open his eyes. . . .

*   *   *

So far, Brick hadn't moved except to turn his head a little to listen. He could still hear the noise. It wasn't loud, and he realized suddenly that he was hearing not just one sound, but many, and that it was coming closer and spreading out around him. Not knowing what it was made him uneasy. It added to a fainter but growing uneasiness that had begun to trouble him from the moment he started asking questions.

Actually, where *was* he? In a real place—or in a little lost world created by five imaginations? And now that he was here —and all alone at that—just what was he going to do? It was rather frightening to remember what Charlie Pill had said. Alone, he was darned near helpless. He doubted if he could even crawl very far.

While he was trying to puzzle out his situation, a grasshopper buzzed up from a tuft of grass on his right and landed on his chest. He'd never seen a real live grasshopper before, though he knew what it was from pictures. But the pictures hadn't told him it could jump so far and make such a racket, and it startled him. In fact, he almost jerked upright, and the only reason he didn't was that he'd long known he couldn't. Even so, he was briefly aware of muscles tightening in him that he'd forgotten about, and he had the very odd feeling that he could wiggle his toes, which he hadn't been able to do for ages.

But these details quickly escaped him as his attention fastened on the grasshopper. It was bright green with touches of brown and yellow, and it had large knowing eyes that seemed to be studying him. It struck him as being a remarkable creature for two reasons: it was just as much alive as he was, and neither he nor Princess nor any of the others had even dreamed of imagining such a thing here.

They had imagined birds and flowers and a warm sun, and the running water he could hear somewhere on his left—but grasshoppers simply hadn't occurred to them. Nor had they thought of including the trees that he could make out through the clearing mist, nor the various strange sounds made by things unknown.

If the grasshopper was real, so were the trees and everything else. This was no imagined spot. It actually existed. But *where?*

Brick could see very little of his surroundings while he lay on his back, so he struggled up on an elbow to get his head above the grass. But before he could fix anything carefully in his mind, he heard the curious sound that had been worrying him all along.

The creature or creatures making it were almost upon him.

In sudden fear he managed to lurch upright. With his movement, the grass about him abruptly exploded with a great thunder of wings, and dozens of feathered bodies hurtled into the air as if they had been shot from guns. It was beyond anything in Brick's experience, and it was so unexpected and terrifying that he cried out in panic and sought blindly to escape.

His fright was like pushing a button. Almost instantly the scene about him faded. In the next breath he was clinging to his bed in the cold darkness of Ward Nine at Belleview.

He couldn't help crying out again, for the sudden switch

from the warm hillside meadow to hated Belleview was as terrifying as the other happening, and in one respect it was worse. For instead of being in his bed he was only partially in it, and was in immediate danger of falling to the hard floor.

He was already slipping when the lights came on, and he heard Nurse Jackson's swift feet approaching. Then her strong hands caught him and lifted him back into bed.

"My goodness, Brick!" she exclaimed, chuckling as she tucked the covers about him. "What were you trying to do? Run away from us?"

In spite of her light tone he knew she was really worried about him. "I—I've already been away," he admitted slowly. "I just now got back."

"You—*what?*"

All the others were awake now, and were beginning to babble questions. Princess was staring at him big-eyed above her pillow. "Did—did you actually *go* there, Brick?" she asked. "To our *place?*"

"I sure did!"

"Honest? To—to our hill with the flowers on it?"

"You bet! And it wasn't anything we'd dreamed up, either. It's real!"

Charlie Pill said, "Phooey! You just had a crazy dream, is all."

"I did not!" Brick protested.

"You did too! You had a nightmare, 'cause I heard you yell. You almost fell out of bed."

"I didn't almost fall out of bed! I mean, that's the way I landed when I came back, and I yelled because I was scared. You'd have been worse than scared! I really went there—and I saw things you wouldn't believe. And—and I'd be there now if something hadn't happened."

"Oh, please tell us about it!" Princess begged. "What happened, Brick?"

"Now hold it, everybody," Nurse Jackson ordered. "Just what's going on here? Brick, you tell me."

Brick drew a deep breath. He didn't mind explaining anything to Nurse Jackson, because they all knew she was on their side. She was older than the day nurses, and in her broad dark face there was a look of wisdom and understanding that the others didn't have. The day nurses didn't like Belleview and were always quitting. But Nurse Jackson stayed on in spite of difficulties. She stayed, Brick knew, only because of Ward Nine. Without her, life would have been unthinkable.

"It—it's like this," he began. "You know that game we play?"

She smiled. "Of course. It's a wonderful game."

"Well, there's this place we've been imagining. It's a peachy spot, sort of on a hillside, with lots of sun and grass and flowers, and a little stream of some kind flowing down on one side. . . ."

"Say, that sounds real nice," Nurse Jackson said approvingly. "I wouldn't mind going there myself."

"That's what we thought we'd try to do. You always said the mind can do anything."

"And it can! If you'd ever seen people get well, when all the doctors said it was impossible . . . But go on, Brick."

"Well, we all kept trying to go there for several nights, and tonight I kept on after everybody had gone to sleep. Then— then all at once I felt the sun on my face, real hot, and I heard a funny noise. And when I opened my eyes, I was there!"

There was a sudden breathless silence around him. He could feel everyone staring at him, waiting. Then Princess whispered, "Wha-what happened next, Brick?" And Lily Rose said, "The funny noise—what was that?"

He told them about the grasshopper, and how the worrisome noise had come closer and closer until he moved, and the grass all around him seemed to explode. "I didn't know it was just a bunch of birds," he went on. "Golly, I was never so scared in my life! All I wanted when it happened was to get away from there. And I did—zing! I landed right back here in bed—or rather on the edge of the bed, because I'd turned somehow and almost missed it."

Again there was an excited silence around him. Then Diz Dobie whispered, "Whew! That was *something!*"

"Aw, I don't believe it," Charlie Pill muttered. "If—if you didn't dream it, you're just making it all up."

"It's the truth," he said quietly. "Everything happened just like I said." He could sort of feel the others' thoughts, and he knew that Charlie wanted desperately to believe it all, but that he was afraid of being disappointed. Poor Charlie couldn't help being a pill, which was one of the reasons they called him that. After all, when you're in pain most of the time—though Charlie seldom admitted he was—you could be excused for a lot of things.

At that moment Brick would have given all he owned—which was only a few old books—for something that would convince Charlie Pill of the truth. He knew that Princess believed him, and that Lily Rose and Diz Dobie did too. Then he glanced at Nurse Jackson. She was still standing at the foot of his bed, looking at him curiously. Her eyes were troubled.

"You—you don't think I was dreaming, do you?" he asked.

"Of course not!" she said stoutly. "I'm sure it happened—and I just wish I could have been along!" She chuckled, but her eyes remained troubled. He suddenly realized that she really wanted to believe him, but that she was even more doubtful than Charlie Pill.

How could he convince her? "Those birds," he began. "The ones that scared me so. I didn't get a good look at them, but they were sort of fat and brown, and they popped up around me like guns going off. What d'you s'pose they were?"

"They sound like quail," Nurse Jackson said thoughtfully. "You must have flushed a big covey of them coming through the grass. Lordy, I haven't seen a covey of quail since—" She stopped and blinked. "Brick, what's that under your neck? I declare if it doesn't look like a leaf!"

For the first time he was aware of something small pressing uncomfortably against the back of his neck, just inside his pajamas. He groped around and got his hand on the thing. It turned out to be a torn bit of a leaf and a crushed yellow flower with some of the petals missing.

"Why, I—I was lying on a whole bunch of flowers like this. I guess, when the birds scared me . . . "

She came slowly over and took the crushed flower with a hand that was not quite steady. "Brick," she said in an awed voice. "Do you know what this is?"

He shook his head. "I never saw one till I found 'em growing all around me at that place."

"Brick, it's a dandelion! But it's winter here, and you won't find one growing anywhere in this part of the country till next spring. Do you realize what this means?"

Charlie Pill gulped excitedly. "I know what it means. It proves he sure enough did go there!"

2

SCOUTING TRIP

By the clock on the opposite wall it was long past midnight, though Brick hardly noticed it. In the sudden realization of what had happened, everybody began to talk at once, and Nurse Jackson sank down into the nearest chair, slowly shaking her head while she stared at the battered dandelion.

"Well!" she said, still shaking her head. "Well! It's almost too much for a poor body to accept—but here's the proof, right here in my hand." She got up and passed the dandelion over to Princess and Lily Rose, who were begging for it. Then she sat down again. "It really gets me," she went on. "The more I think about it, the more it gets me. Brick, you actually *teleported!*"

"I—what?" he said uncertainly, wondering about the word.

"You teleported. That's what you did. I've read of it being done, but I never believed it till now. I sure wish I knew where you went! Have you any idea?"

"It—it was to that place we'd been imagining," he told her. "That's all I know. Only, it's not an imaginary place at all. It's absolutely *real.*"

"Oh, I don't doubt that for an instant," she said quickly. "You brought back an absolutely real dandelion, and I'm sure the birds and the grasshopper you saw were just as real. But where is this place? Somehow I think it's important to know."

She paused, then asked, "Brick, what else did you see besides what you've told us?"

"Why, I—I'm not sure. It all happened so quickly. And the grass was so high I couldn't see much, except right in front of me. I was on the side of a little hill, it seemed like. Some of the flowers were different. I mean, they had white petals and long stems. . . . "

"Probably daisies," said Nurse Jackson. "What about trees? Did you notice any?"

Brick frowned. "Why, I did see some trees! I've just remembered. They were over on the other hill, just across that little stream. But things were sort of misty and I couldn't tell much about 'em."

"Misty?" Princess echoed curiously. "It was misty over there?"

"Well, a little. I mean, it seemed to be clearing because the sun was just cutting through it, real warm and bright. It was so bright it was dazzling."

Everyone was silent a moment. Suddenly Charlie Pill burst out, "The whole thing's crazy! It just now hit me. Can't you see how crazy it is?"

"What's so crazy about it?"

"Why, the sun! Don't you get it? The sun! It's in the middle of the night here—but where you went it's bright daylight!"

"What of it?" said Princess. "That's no crazier than going from winter to summer. I think it's wonderful!"

"It's wonderful," Nurse Jackson affirmed, "but it *is* sort of crazy. I just can't figure it out." She carried the dandelion from Lily Rose to Diz Dobie, then sat down and shook her head again. "Brick," she went on, "at first I thought you'd teleported to some place in the South. Georgia, maybe, or even Florida. That would explain the flowers and the warm sun. And also the quail. But if it's night here, it would be night there too. It would be night everywhere except on the other side of the globe, in Europe and Asia."

She stopped, then said, "I'd sure like to pin this down. Brick, think hard. Was the sun almost overhead when you saw it?"

"Not quite. It was just a little to my left."

"H'mm. Without knowing directions, there's no telling whether it was morning or afternoon. But it does rule out most of Europe. As nearly as I can remember, it would be early morning in France, but much later to the east. Say around noon as we get to India, and maybe afternoon in China."

"I wasn't in India or China," Brick said. "I'm sure of that."

"What makes you so sure?" Charlie Pill asked. "Man, you could have been *anywhere!*"

"But not India or China. I was somewhere in America. I *felt* it."

"But—but you *couldn't* have been! It's night all over America!"

There was an abrupt silence in the ward. Brick managed to struggle up on his elbows—it was a new position he didn't immediately realize he'd taken—and looked around at the others. On his right, just beyond the thrust-aside screen, Princess and Lily Rose were staring at him tensely, eyes wide with wonder. Without great effort neither girl could do more than turn her head toward him, nor could Charlie Pill on his left, who was all skin and bones. Only Diz Dobie, who was stronger than any of them, was able to force himself over on his side. The brown boy had given the dandelion to Charlie and was now trying to speak, but as usual seemed unable to find words.

Suddenly Princess exclaimed, "What difference does it make where it is? Maybe it's on the other side of the moon—but who cares?" Then she added wistfully, "Oh, I've just got to go there! I've just *got* to."

"I've got to go, too!" Lily Rose said quickly. "If Brick can do it, I'm sure the rest of us can."

"Sure we can!" Diz Dobie echoed. "Golly, let's—let's try it right now!"

"Now wait a minute," Nurse Jackson cautioned. "I don't want any of you to try anything until we've talked this over a little more. That place may sound nice, but it could be dangerous. Just because Brick managed to go there and return safely doesn't mean everyone could do it. Suppose you got over on that hill—but couldn't get back?"

"I wouldn't care in the least," Princess said dreamily. "Why, I'd just lie right there on a bed of dandelions till I died. Sunshine and flowers . . ."

The nurse shook her head. "Let's not get carried away," she reminded them. "I'm all for sunshine and flowers myself, but we have to be practical about this. Brick, you were on that hillside only a few minutes, but I'm sure you learned more than you realize. It's just a matter of my asking you the right questions. Now, think back. What sounds did you hear?"

He closed his eyes and slid down upon his pillow. "There was the funny noise those—those quail were making, then there was the grasshopper—he made a sort of clickity buzz. I remember now that I heard more grasshoppers in the distance, only I didn't realize what they were at the time. There were some birds chirping or singing somewhere, and there was the water on my left. That was the main sound. I couldn't see the water till I got my head up and looked down at the bottom of the hill, but I could hear it flowing. It was sort of gurgling, only it was more like music. It sure was nice."

The silence that followed was broken by a wistful sigh from Princess. Then Nurse Jackson said, "But Brick, those were all nature sounds. Didn't you hear anything else? Traffic in the distance? A factory whistle? And what about machinery humming or clanking, or maybe a car's horn?"

He shook his head. "There was nothing like that."

"How about a radio, or a plane?"

"No, ma'am."

"No sounds of people?"

"I—I didn't hear a thing except what I've told you. It was, well, a real quiet place. Honest, I didn't know a place could be so quiet."

"That's strange. Didn't you see any signs of people?"

"I sure didn't."

"But, Brick, people are practically everywhere. You can't go anywhere without seeing signs of them. Tin cans, bottles, old tires, trash . . ."

He shook his head.

"There has to be something," she insisted. "If you were 'way out in the country, there'd be other signs. Barns, sheds, fences —you just can't get away from fences . . ."

He started to shake his head again, then frowned instead. "I'm not sure, but maybe I *did* see something. It was just a— a sort of quick glimpse, so I don't know what it was. I—I was so surprised at being there instead of here that I didn't even think about it at the time. But—"

"Can you remember what it was—what it looked like?"

"I'll try. Maybe—"

Suddenly, before he could recall what he'd seen, he was interrupted by the door to the main corridor being thrust open. Miss Preedy, the night supervisor, entered the ward. She was a tall, severe woman who spoke sweetly, but Brick had learned that the sweetness was only a thin veneer over what seemed to be unbending metal.

"What seems to be going on in here?" Miss Preedy demanded in her most sugary tone. "Having a little midnight party, are we?"

"Oh, somebody just cried out in his sleep and woke up the others," Nurse Jackson said easily. "But everything's all right now."

"I see. And what is the screen doing open? Haven't I said it was to be kept closed at night? Rules are rules, Miss Jackson, and I expect them to be obeyed." Miss Preedy always ignored the fact that Nurse Jackson was a widow.

"Yes, ma'am. But it had to be opened so I could check on things."

"Well, close it immediately," Miss Preedy ordered. "I never approved of such an arrangement, but it couldn't be helped in an old place like this. It'll certainly be a relief when we finish moving to the new building. At least we can place the children around in some up-to-date wards, though one or two will have to be sent . . ."

She shrugged and started out, but paused briefly to add over her shoulder, "And leave the door open, Miss Jackson. The ward doors should never be closed."

Brick was stunned. He'd heard that some of Belleview's patients—he understood they were just the very old people— were being moved to a new place on the edge of the city. But no one had told him they'd all have to go, and that their group would be broken up. When that happened they might never see each other again.

There was a stifled sob on his right, and he heard Lily Rose whimper, "Wha-what are we going to do if they s-separate us?"

"Now, honey, don't you worry about that," Nurse Jackson said quickly. "They haven't separated you yet, and if they ever try it, it'll be over my dead body."

Her broad black face had become grimly stony. Defiantly leaving the screen open, she went over to the door and snapped out the lights, then peered searchingly into the corridor. Returning, she sat down again and said in a low voice, "Miss Preedy, she was just talking to hear herself talk. The truth is, they don't really know what they're going to do with you. If they'd decided anything, I'd have found out and told you, but they just don't know. You see, there's no place to put you.

Somebody goofed on the new building and forgot to make space for you, and over at the Children's Hospital they're splitting at the seams. So you'll have to stay here."

"But—but isn't Belleview condemned?" Brick asked.

She chuckled. "It was condemned five years ago, but it's still creaking along." She paused a moment, then asked quietly, "Brick, have you remembered what you saw before that covey of quail scared you?"

"Well, sort of."

"What do you mean, 'sort of'?"

"Well, I remember what it looked like, but I don't know what it was."

"Oh, tell us!" Princess whispered excitedly. "Tell us all about it!"

"There's not much to tell. It was over on the other hill, on the edge of the trees, and I only saw it for a second before it was blotted out in the mist. At first I thought it was a wall, a high stone wall. I mean, that was the impression I got before the mist covered it. But it could have been some sort of building, a long low one. Or it might have been a shed, or even a fence made of wood. I—I just don't know. Anyway, I'm sure going back for a better look at it."

He raised up on his elbows and glanced at their dim faces on either side. "How about it? Do you all want to try it again and see if we can make it together?"

*　　*　　*

They tried it, and they tried hard, but it was no use. The hour was far too late, and they were exhausted. Brick was sure he almost made it, for there was a brief moment when he felt the sun's warmth on his face. But it faded on the instant, and when he opened his tired eyes he found he was still in his bed in Ward Nine. Nurse Jackson had left, and by the sound of their breathing he knew the others had fallen to sleep.

Disappointed, he drifted wearily away into a series of troubled dreams in which he seemed to be trying desperately to open a locked door. It was terribly important that he open it, but though he tried dozens and dozens of keys, none of them would fit.

When he opened his eyes again it was morning and almost time for breakfast.

Everything was strangely late that morning. Instead of one of the ever-hurried day nurses finally coming to take care of them, it was Nurse Jackson herself.

"What's happened?" Brick asked worriedly, knowing instinctively that something was wrong. "Why are you still on duty?"

"Oh, we're a little shorthanded," she said easily. "I just offered to help out. After all, you folks are my special family."

But there was more to it than that, and Brick was very much aware of it. The others were too. Usually after breakfast they were wheeled to the therapy room and given exercise and a massage. Today, however, no one came for them, and even lunch was more than an hour late. When Nurse Jackson at last managed to bring it, Brick was surprised to see that it was only a tray of sandwiches which she divided among them on paper napkins.

"The kitchen's closed down for a while," she told them. "I'm sure they'll have it working by tomorrow, but in the meantime it looks like sandwiches for all of us."

When she had gone, Brick said, "There's something awfully funny going on. She's really worried."

"She's worried about us," Princess said. "I got that much without even trying to tune in."

"Maybe we all ought to tune in together and find out what's happening," he suggested. "How about it, gang?"

"Yeah," said Charlie Pill. "I think we'd better."

The others agreed. No one wanted to do it, but they decided

they must, so they closed their eyes and pretended they were radio receivers tuning in on all the main thoughts being silently broadcast throughout Belleview. It was much easier than playing the traveling game, and in the beginning they'd had a lot of fun with it among themselves. But it was no fun at all when they tuned in on the people beyond Ward Nine. For ugly old Belleview was a place of pain and poverty and misery, and even those who worked here hated it.

Brick wasn't surprised when he suddenly heard Lily Rose crying. In some ways she was the most sensitive of them, more so even than Princess, who was the most imaginative. "I—I just can't stand it," Lily Rose said tearfully. "All those poor people!"

"Aw, they're no poorer than anybody," Brick said practically. "You tuned in on those old drunks—they're all broken-down from drinking, and now they're feeling sorry for themselves because they're not allowed to have any liquor. What'd you pick up, Charlie?"

"People are being moved out fast," Charlie Pill told him. "A lot faster than they'd planned. But I don't know why."

"I—I know why," Diz Dobie said.

"Let's have it," Brick ordered impatiently. The brown boy had them all beat when it came to tuning in, but he sure wasn't much on talk.

"Well," Diz Dobie answered slowly, "this building, it's been condemned. They're gonna tear it down."

"Aw, we know all that," Brick muttered. "It's ancient history. But the place is still here, and I'll bet it'll keep on being here for a long time to come."

"No, it won't. It—it's been re-condemned. They—they got orders first thing this morning to hurry to get everybody out of here by tomorrow night. Then they're gonna start wrecking the place immediately."

"Oh, lordy!"

Shock held them silent a moment. Then Brick said, "All I could get was that the kitchen is closed down, and that the people who work in it have either quit or gone over to the new building. And I think some of the nurses want to go on strike because of poor pay. But I didn't pick up a thing about us."

"I did," Princess said quietly. "It's just as Nurse Jackson said. Somebody goofed on the plans, and now they can't find room for us anywhere. They want us out, but they don't know what to do with us. And—and Nurse Jackson's worried sick about us because anything can happen, and we'll probably be separated."

"Oh, no!" Lily Rose wailed. "We can't let them do that to us!"

"I don't know how we can stop 'em," Charlie Pill grumbled.

Brick said, "We ought to be able to think of something."

They were silent a moment. Then suddenly Princess exclaimed, "I've got it! It's the most *wonderful* idea!"

Charlie Pill turned his head and looked at her sourly. "Yeah? I know what you're thinking, and it's crazy. You're thinking we should all join hands, close our eyes, say 'Presto,' and go zipping over to that place of Brick's. Sure, and what d'you expect us to do when we get there? Spend the rest of our lives flopping around on those goofy flowers?" He gave a derisive snort. "Now I ask you, who's gonna take care of us and feed us?"

"Stupid, we'll take Nurse Jackson with us, of course!"

"Yeah? And what about our beds, and maybe a tent to keep off the rain, and a truck full of food . . ."

"Charlie Pill, you're in*suff*erable! Why, you haven't a bit of imagination. Once we get over there, I just know we can work things out. Don't you think so, Brick?"

Brick didn't answer at once. He'd suddenly found he could wiggle his toes, and it was such an amazing discovery that it left him momentarily speechless. He hadn't had a bit of feeling in his body since that long-ago day at the orphanage when one of the big guys had pushed him down the stairs. But now, incredibly, feeling was coming back. Why? Could his trip to the dandelion place have had anything to do with it? It had to be that. Come to think of it, just before the birds scared him over there, he'd somehow felt he could wiggle his toes if he tried. The act of teleporting must have re-connected something that had long been torn apart.

If going to the dandelion place could make him well again, wouldn't it do the same for the others?

"Brick!" Princess was saying. "What's the matter with you? I asked you a question. Didn't you hear me?"

"I—I heard you," he said slowly. "And I—I think you've got a great idea. It's the answer to everything."

Charlie Pill gaped at him. "Have you lost your ever-loving mind?"

Brick laughed. "Watch!" he said.

He thrust the bedcovers aside. It took far more effort than he'd thought, but he managed to raise one foot and to move it a little. The others gaped at him, and a tired Nurse Jackson, entering the ward at that moment, almost dropped the evening tray of sandwiches that she was carrying.

"Brick!" she gasped. "What are you *doing?*"

He laughed again and explained what he believed had happened to him by going to the dandelion place. "If it helped me," he told her, "it ought to help us all. As soon as we've eaten I'm going back—and I want everyone to try to come with me."

Nurse Jackson gave a sad little sigh. "I sure wish you'd known about this weeks ago. Have you heard what's going on here?"

Princess said gaily, "Oh, we heard all about it, but it doesn't matter now. If they want everybody out by tomorrow night, we'll just fool 'em and vanish—and we'll take you with us and never come back. You—you'll come with us, won't you?"

The nurse rolled her eyes. "Of course I'd come with you if

I could. My man's dead, and my poor boy was killed in the last war. So you're the only family I've got. But honey—" She shook her head wearily and began distributing the sandwiches. "Honey, you just don't understand. You've been in bed so long, you haven't learned about the practical side of life. You can't go to a strange place empty-handed and expect to live. Why, old Danny Boone himself would think twice before he tried it!"

Brick stammered, "But—but it won't hurt to scout it out first. We'd have to do that. Please, will you roll our beds closer together so we can hold hands?"

"Hold hands for what?"

Charlie Pill said, "Ha! They've got the crazy idea it'll be easier to go to that place together if we all hold hands."

"Well, maybe it would," Nurse Jackson admitted. She thrust the beds together and said, "If I had better sense, I'd talk you out of it. But I'm just too beat. I've had only an hour's sleep since last night, so I'm going back to my cot to get some more. If you need me, just press the call button and I'll wake right up."

*   *   *

Brick did not think to study the clock as he prepared for the scouting trip. The early dark had come, and falling snow was muffling the eternal roar of traffic outside. He was hardly aware of it. Though the narrow beds had been thrust as closely to-gether as possible, the service tables between them kept them apart, and it was all he could do to touch the outstretched hands on either side. He was forced to shift to the right so that small Princess could reach him and keep a tight grip on one of his fingers, but this made it harder for Charlie Pill.

Charlie Pill muttered, "I still think this is crazy. I don't see how holding hands—"

"Stop thinking how crazy it is," Brick ordered, "and keep your mind on the dandelion place."

Diz Dobie said, "It oughta work if we hang on. It's like—like hooking up batteries."

"That's right," said Brick. "Only they're mental batteries. Now everybody concentrate. . . ."

"How—how long do you think it will take?" Lily Rose whispered.

"I don't know. Maybe an hour."

"I can't hang on for an hour," said Charlie Pill.

"Then hang on for as long as you can. Now *concentrate!*"

Time surely passed, though for long it seemed to be standing still. Brick wasn't aware of the exact moment when Ward Nine vanished and there was a change, but all at once he realized he was somewhere else, and at the same moment he heard Princess cry out in fright.

He opened his eyes and gasped.

Something had gone very wrong.

3

THE CURIOUS BUILDING

He seemed to be lying on the grass as before, but instead of that wonderfully bright sun overhead to warm him, the sky was dark, and a chill breeze was cutting through his pajamas. Worse, the ground about him was damp and cold. He could feel the coldness seeping straight into his backbone. He'd lost contact with everyone, though he was aware of Princess somewhere on his right.

"Brick?" he heard her cry tremulously. "Brick? Where are you?"

"I'm right here."

He stretched out his arm as far as he could reach, and instantly a small searching hand clasped his and clung to it for comfort.

"Oh, thank goodness! I'm so glad I found you! Where are we, Brick? Oh, this is awful! Wha-what's happened?"

"I—I don't know." Then he called, "Charlie? Diz? Lily Rose? Hey, where is everybody?"

There was no answer. He fought down the fear clutching at him and managed to say, "We—we must have left 'em all behind. I—I just can't figure . . ."

"I—I'm so c-cold, Brick. And I—I'm scared. I'd rather be back in Ward Nine than in this horrible p-place!"

"Okay. I'll take you back. But wait just a minute. . . ."

In spite of the dark and the cold, something about the spot where he was lying had a familiar feel. He was on a slope just as before, and close on his left there was the same pleasant music of running water. There were some strange sounds, like those curious tick-tockings and peepings somewhere below him, but he could hear a few birds in the distance. Their sleepy twitterings made him wonder if they could just be waking up.

Was it nearly dawn here? And could it be possible that this was the same place he'd come to before? All at once he knew it had to be. But what had gone wrong?

Suddenly he realized what had happened.

"Hey!" he cried, as he struggled up on his elbows. "This is the right place after all! We just came too early."

"I—I don't understand," Princess said uncertainly.

"But it's simple. I forgot the difference in time. You see, when I first came here, it was after midday—but it was after midnight back at Ward Nine. That means there's about twelve hours difference between where we are and where we were. Do you get it?"

"I think so. If—if we left there at five o'clock in the evening, it would be about five in the morning here."

"That's it. So it shouldn't be long—" He caught his breath, and burst out excitedly, *"Will you look at that!"*

The sky had brightened, and on the right it was turning a brilliant red. Then the entire horizon seemed to burst into flame. It was as if there'd been a vast explosion that had set the world on fire. It was awesome and frightening and beautiful and incredible—and it was absolutely soundless, save for the now-awakened birds. And suddenly, as he stared, a monstrous molten ball of gleaming gold slid upward and flung its brilliance over the land.

Princess whispered ecstatically, "The *sun! It's the sun!*"

Brick clutched the grass and blinked at it until its growing brightness forced him to turn his eyes away. He was overwhelmed. Until now, the grimy buildings of the city had bounded their world and had shut out all horizons. This was the first sunrise they had ever seen.

"Boy!" he said finally. "Boy o' boy! I sure never dreamed it could look like that!"

Without realizing what he'd done, he found he'd somehow managed to sit upright. Though it was tiring, it raised his eye level well above the grass, and he was able to see everything he had missed before. He braced himself with his arms and peered curiously about, filled with the wonder of a world that was so different from all he had ever known.

They were on the edge of a bowl-shaped meadow tucked between low, forested hills. Immediately on the left, he could make out the tiny stream he had been hearing. It went tumbling down through a carpet of dandelions and other flowers to the foot of the opposite hill, where it was joined by another small spring flowing in from the right. After the first careful glance about him, his attention went quickly to the spot where he had briefly glimpsed something on his first visit.

At the moment, he could make out nothing. It was too early, and the misty woods on the other hill were still deep in shadow. As he squinted at the trees, trying vainly to see through them, the mounting sun brightened the distant edge of the meadow on the left and outlined three animals grazing there. One was a great black horse with a long mane. Near it were two deer —a slender doe with a fawn.

He glanced eagerly at Princess, and found that she, too, had managed to sit up and was looking with wide-eyed fascination at the animals.

"They're so *beautiful!*" she whispered breathlessly. "Oh, I wish I could go over and pet them. I believe I could if I tried."

He was astounded when Princess actually got to her feet and took several faltering steps down the slope. Then she collapsed.

He crawled over to her. "Are—are you all right?"

For a few seconds she seemed unable to speak. Then she stammered, "D-did you see me? I *walked!* I actually *walked!*"

"You sure did! I'll bet everybody can do it if we can just get 'em over here."

"Maybe we ought to go back and get them," she suggested happily. "Shall we?"

"Not yet. We'd better find out all we can about this place while we're here."

He glanced in the direction of the animals, and was almost relieved to see them moving away downstream. The deer were probably safe enough, but the horse wasn't exactly his idea of Black Beauty. The huge creature impressed him as being absolutely wild.

Again his attention went to the woods on the other side of the meadow. The mist was clearing under the warm sun, and now he could trace a vague shape back in the shadows.

"Look!" he said, pointing. "That's what I saw the first time I came here. That long dark thing—it looks like it's on the other side of the trees. What is it?"

"I see it," Princess said in a low voice. "I believe it's a house."

"If it's a house, it's sure got a funny shape. It stretches 'way off to the left."

"Brick, that's a fence on the left."

"It's doggone high for a fence. It's more like a stockade. You know, the kind we're always seeing around a fort in one of those westerns on TV."

"Oh, Brick, maybe it *is* a fort with a stockade! Wouldn't it just boggle you to find we were actually 'way out West somewhere, with Indians and cowboys and settlers and soldiers—"

"Yeah," he muttered. "It sure would, because it's impossible. Don't you realize that's all Hollywood make-believe? This is for real."

"Then where *are* we?"

He shrugged. "That's what really boggles me. I can't figure it. But if I can get over to that house or fort, or whatever it is yonder, maybe I can find out."

By using great care and effort, he managed to stand up as Princess had done and take a few faltering steps. But his long-unused legs were too weak to support him, and abruptly he crumpled. Then he saw that Princess was on her hands and knees, crawling. He tried it, and found it fairly easy, except that they both had to stop every few feet and rest.

The sun was hot on their backs now, and it was a great relief when they finally reached the little spring at the foot of the slope and buried their faces in the cold sweet water. It was the best water Brick had ever tasted.

Princess said finally, "My, that was good! But I'm afraid I can't go any farther. I—I'm just too tired."

Brick was tired, too, and he was dismayed when he glanced over at the slope ahead. Though it was a gentle slope, carpeted with flowers like the one behind him, he doubted if he could make it to the top. Yet he had to try. Something told him that the most important thing in the world was to reach that building and find out everything he could about it.

"I've just got to go on," he told Princess. "Only, I don't like to leave you here all alone."

"Oh, but I won't be alone," she said happily. "There are thousands of unspeakably wonderful things everywhere around me. I could spend days and days right here, just looking."

"Well, if anything happens before I get back, all you have to do is think real hard of your bed in Ward Nine, and you'll be back there in no time."

*   *   *

It must have taken him nearly an hour to crawl painfully up to the trees, a comparatively short distance which anyone with good legs could have covered in seconds. The most awkward part was crossing the spring. The ground was too boggy on the right to attempt going around it, but he managed to sort of sprawl and flop to the other side without getting anything wet but the lower parts of his pajamas and his feet.

Just before entering the trees, he stopped and glanced back at Princess, but she was so absorbed in something in the water that she did not see him. He was very tired now, and if his goal hadn't been clearly in sight, he might have thought twice about going on. But there it was, just a little way ahead. A low stone building with a thatched roof, and it was built at one corner of what seemed to be a long stockade.

Sudden excitement rose in him. He forgot his weariness and went scrambling through the trees as fast as he could move. What parts of the world had stone houses with thatched roofs? The only place he could think of was Ireland.

Ireland?

He stopped a moment in sheer surprise. Was Ireland far enough around the world to explain the difference in time? And what about the trees? These looked like pictures he'd seen of pines, but they were awfully big, and some of them had slashes in the bark with odd-looking cups fastened to them. Did the Irish have pines like these? But what of the stockade? Somehow he had the idea that the Irish built stone walls instead.

Could this be Russia—or Siberia? Still, the climate . . .

A little chill came over him, and he looked intently at the structure and realized it wasn't a stockade after all. It was a very high fence made of slender poles placed about a foot apart. In between, near the ground, were short pieces that made the lower part of the fence practically solid. Was it built that way to keep something out—or in?

As he began crawling forward again, cautiously now, Brick found himself unconsciously listening—listening for some sound that would indicate the presence of people. Instead, he was again impressed by the quiet. Other than the small sounds of birds and insects, it was so very quiet that the sudden chattering of a squirrel overhead gave him a momentary fright. Squirrels, like the brown lizards and yellow butterflies he had already noticed, were creatures he had never seen except in pictures, and ordinarily he would have been enthralled by them. But the strange building ahead demanded all his attention.

He pressed forward with a sort of cautious eagerness, and seconds later he was crouched before a curiously carved wooden door.

Brick peered up at it almost in disbelief. Somebody had spent a lot of time carving that door, for it was covered with a design of interlocking squares of all sizes. Even the wooden mechanism that served as an outside latch was part of the decoration.

Now, why would anyone put that much work on a door—especially for a place as remote as this? Then he saw that every detail of the structure, including the many-paned window on the left, was just as carefully designed and made.

What was inside?

As he studied the door, he realized it didn't have a lock. Anyone could open it by raising the latch.

Brick argued with himself a moment, wondering if it would be wrong to enter, but he quickly decided it wouldn't be. He *had* to get inside so he could learn all he could and report it to the others.

By grasping the cut stones framing the entrance, he managed to get to his feet and cling there long enough to raise the latch. He had a few seconds of trouble when he discovered that the heavy door opened outward instead of inward, but presently he was crawling inside, blinking with astonishment at the broad room before him.

It was much larger than he had expected, with a great

fireplace on the right and double bunks of old carved wood lining two walls. An immense long table with benches around it occupied the center of the place. Most of the far wall beyond it was taken up by a broad window, but from where he crouched he couldn't see what was on the other side. His amazed eyes roved about, taking in the carved wood, the tools and musical instruments hanging from pegs, the strings of dried onions and corn dangling from the beams overhead, and the polished cooking things in the alcove by the fireplace. Everything here, including the stone floor beneath him, was old and worn, but carefully preserved and shiningly clean.

Only the faint film of dust on the flagstones gave evidence that no one had used the place for a long time.

Brick was puzzling over that, and wondering why it hadn't been locked, when he heard a rush of wind outside and the big carved door suddenly banged shut.

For a moment he stared at it uncertainly, feeling he had somehow made a mistake. Then with rising uneasiness he crawled over to it and tried to push it open.

The heavy door refused to budge.

Now he remembered how the stone casing outside was slotted to engage the wooden mechanism, and he realized the door would automatically bolt itself when closed. He struggled to his feet and began tugging and twisting the wooden handle that was part of the inside design. It should have released the bolt on the outside—but it didn't. Feverishly he pulled and twisted, trying everything he could think of, but the door would not open. He was trapped.

Under this awful realization he sank exhausted to the floor. What a crazy door! Whoever built it must have been off his rocker, because the mechanism with the bolt should have been on the inside.

What was he going to do?

He was so tired by now that he could not help closing his

eyes a moment and wishing he had a place to rest a while, a comfortable bed somewhere. Unconsciously, as he did so, he visioned his own bed in Ward Nine. . . .

This time, because he wanted so desperately to be out of his prison, the change came almost instantly.

*   *   *

He hadn't been ready to return, and it was a shock to suddenly find himself huddled on his bed in the same position he had been in on the flagstone floor. He straightened and swung about and looked wildly around. The lights were on, and Nurse Jackson, who apparently had just entered the ward, was standing frozen near the door, staring at him as if she had never seen him before. He realized the others were staring too, and were babbling questions, but his attention was on the bed to his right.

It was empty.

Lily Rose, half in tears, asked plaintively, "What's happened to Princess?"

"Oh, lordy," Nurse Jackson gasped. "I pray to heaven she's all right. I should never have allowed you—" She came swiftly over to his bed. "Brick, what in the world—How did you get so dirty?"

He swallowed and said, "I—I didn't mean to come back without her. It was an accident. I mean, we'd crawled down to that little stream—"

Charlie Pill said, "Are you nuts? You know Princess can't crawl! Why, she can hardly move—"

"She can crawl now," he told Charlie. "She can even walk. I can, too. I—"

"*Walk?*" Nurse Jackson whispered.

"Yeah, but not far. Give us a few days to get used to it, and I'll bet—"

"But what *happened*, Brick?"

"Well, as I was saying, she was too tired to go on when we reached that little stream. So I left her there and crawled on up to that building I saw. Only, when I got inside, the wind blew the door shut, and it locked on me. I couldn't get out."

"So you teleported back here?"

"Well, that's what happened, only I didn't intend it that way."

Nurse Jackson frowned. "And Princess is waiting where you left her?"

Brick nodded. "I—I'm sure she's all right. We got there too early—it was still dark, and without a blanket it was awfully cold till the sun came up. But that sun's hot, and she was sitting right out in it. . . . "

" *'Sitting right out in it?'* " Nurse Jackson repeated, aghast. "Brick, don't you know what the sun will do to her? Why, that poor little pale thing, she's never been exposed to it in her life! Her skin's so tender it could kill her!"

"But she can come back here any time she wishes. I told her how."

Lily Rose said in a small voice, "Maybe she can't, alone. None of us here could go over there alone. We've been trying. Maybe, if everybody could have hung on to each other's hand . . . "

"But we couldn't," said Charlie Pill. "We just gave out. You know what I think? It sure gets me, but I think Brick's the only guy who can go to that place. And when he goes, I'm thinking he can take only one of us at a time."

"I believe Charlie's right," said Lily Rose.

"Me too," said Diz Dobie.

"Oh, dear!" Nurse Jackson seemed to have forgotten the tray she had been holding all the while. Suddenly she ordered, "Brick, you get yourself over to that dandelion place fast and bring that poor girl back here!"

Before he could answer, Miss Preedy, the night supervisor,

appeared in the doorway. Brick glimpsed her in the nick of time and managed to flip the bedclothes over himself before he was seen. It would never do to have her start asking questions he couldn't easily answer, or to have her even suspect he was regaining the use of a body that long had been paralyzed. If she did, she'd pack him off fast to one of the children's homes, and that would really put the fix to things.

"What in the world," Miss Preedy began sweetly, "are all the beds doing jammed together like this? Explain that, Miss Jackson."

"Don't ask me to explain anything," Nurse Jackson replied with equal sweetness. "I just now got in here, and I've been on duty ever since—"

"And where's that pale girl?" Miss Preedy interrupted, looking down her long nose at the empty bed. "Don't tell me they found a place for her in the new building!"

Nurse Jackson sighed. "I doubt it. She must have been moved by mistake. I wouldn't be a bit surprised to see her back here any minute."

"I hope not. It would be one less patient to worry about. And Miss Jackson, the lights should have been out six minutes ago. We mustn't waste taxpayers' money. And what have I said about that screen? Rules are rules, and as long as we are here, I expect them to be obeyed."

The moment Miss Preedy was safely away from the ward, Nurse Jackson closed the door and ordered, "Get going, Brick! Hurry!"

Brick swallowed. He was so tired from all his exertions that he had grave doubts of his ability to go anywhere for a while. As for returning immediately with another person . . . "Please," he began, "if I can make it—and I'll do my best—I don't know when I can get back. So maybe I'd better take some blankets or something along for protection."

Nurse Jackson went swiftly to the cabinet in the far corner

and returned with a pair of gray blankets. She folded them tightly and tucked them under his arms.

"Try hard," she said urgently. "And good luck!"

Brick closed his eyes and concentrated. He figured he might as well save himself all the extra effort he could, so he directed his thoughts upon the spot near the spring where he had seen Princess last.

Now, as before, time seemed to stand still. Possibly it was his concern for Princess that overcame his weakness and gave him the force he needed. It is also likely that he was finding it easier to use his newly discovered ability. Whatever the reason, he was all at once aware of a change, and suddenly he felt the hot sun beating down on him.

He opened his eyes, and found he was exactly where he had wished to be.

But Princess was not where he had left her. She was nowhere in sight.

4

FLIGHT

Brick sat up, feeling a sudden cold clutching of uneasiness, and looked quickly around. The uneasiness changed to fear. The fear mounted and stabbed him to his knees, and finally to his feet. He was not immediately aware that much of his weariness had vanished, and that he could actually stand with very little effort. All his thoughts were on Princess. She was like a sister to him, a younger sister who had always looked up to him and whom he had to protect. If anything had happened to her . . .

Again and again, more frantically each time, his eyes searched the length and breadth of the meadow, the windings of the brook running through it, and the edges of the surrounding woods. There was no sign of Princess anywhere.

He was almost afraid to call out for her. His tortured imagination was conjuring a succession of dangers that might be lurking in the shadows of the woods. This was a strange land, totally unknown. Why, the people who had constructed the curious building might be savage barbarians, or even vicious humanoids of the kind he'd once read about in a science-fiction story. If they hadn't found Princess and captured her, maybe she'd been dragged away and devoured by a bloodthirsty beast, say a saber-toothed tiger. The country really did look wild.

He ran an unsteady hand through his thatch of dark-red hair, then tugged on it as if to straighten out his thoughts. This was no time to let his imagination run away with him. He had to be practical. Suddenly it occurred to him that possibly, just possibly, she'd grown tired of waiting for him, or had begun to worry, and had decided to follow him to the building.

Once more he studied the slope on the other side of the spring. Then, in despair, he remembered how long it had taken him to reach the trees. Could Princess have crawled that far since he'd last seen her? Considering how little strength she had, it didn't seem possible.

As he felt the hot sun biting through his flimsy pajamas, he wondered if there was a shady hiding place close by which she might have crawled into and gone to sleep. There were bushes and shrubs scattered all along the main brook. As his eyes swung slowly to the right, he saw, just above the boggy ground from which the spring flowed, a clump of low shrubs overgrown with vines. Was that something white under the leaves?

"Princess!" he cried, and went stumbling toward her.

He didn't make it on his feet, but presently he crawled into a leafy cave, shady and cool and comfortable with matted grass. Princess was sound asleep as he entered, but when he spoke her name again, she stirred and sat up, rubbing her eyes.

"Golly, you sure had me scared!" he said. "I didn't see you when I got back and I thought something had run off with you."

"It was too hot," she explained. "Oh, I love the sun, but I've heard that too much of it at first can hurt people, so I came here." Then, her eyes suddenly bright with curiosity, she asked tensely, "Brick, what did you find up at that place?"

When he had told her all that had happened, she exclaimed, "Oh, I've just got to see that house! If you'll help me, I'm sure I can get up there! Please, Brick—"

"No. It's time we went back to Ward Nine. Nurse Jackson said—"

"But I don't want to go back! I never want to see that place again."

"But—but you can't stay here! Not by yourself!"

"Of course I can! Anyway, I wouldn't be alone very long. It won't take you any time to go to Ward Nine and get the others."

As he stared at her, she added quickly, "And don't tell me we haven't a place to stay. Didn't you say that house has bunks in it? If it's open and not being used, I'm sure nobody—"

"Princess," he interrupted, "we don't know anything about the people who own that house. What if they're humanoids or something?"

"Oh, pooh! What if they are? I'll take them to Miss Preedy. Anyway, humanoids *could* be fun, 'specially if they spoke nothing but music and came in bright colors." Her voice dropped to a whisper. "Brick, do—do you 'spose we're in another world?"

"I'll be jiggered if I know. This could be Siberia."

"Oh, no! Siberia is always yards and yards deep in snow, 'specially now. This is a *warm* place. I love it, and I'm going to stay here. And you've got to hurry and bring the others before they are moved. Why, it would be the awfullest thing if we were separated and never saw each other again, and they never had a chance to get well." She stopped and looked at him earnestly. "Brick, you—you're not afraid to live here, are you?"

"Afraid? Naw! But we've got to be practical. We'll need clothes and things. And what about food?"

"Oh, we could have Nurse Jackson bring clothes for us. And we couldn't possibly go hungry. This is an—an absolutely magical place. Look!"

She held up something that looked like a ripe strawberry, then pressed it into his mouth. "Eat it," she ordered.

He could count on the fingers of one hand the number of times he'd eaten strawberries in Ward Nine. It was whispered, in fact, that more of the taxpayers' money went into private pockets at Belleview than into food. This strawberry was like no other he'd ever tasted.

"Wow!" he exclaimed. "Where'd you get it?"

"Why, they're all over the place! I'm surprised you didn't notice them. There must be bushels and bushels growing wild all along the brook."

The thought of so many wild berries, free for the picking, wiped away his last concern. He didn't know much about the outdoors, but he figured if one kind of food grew wild, there'd be other kinds as well.

"Okay," he said. "I'll go back and get the others. But you'd better come with me. You'll have to talk to them. They'll want to hear your side of it as well as mine—Nurse Jackson especially."

"Brick, I—I hate to go back. I've an awful feeling about it."

"But you've *got* to go. You know that."

"I—I s'pose so."

"Then hang on to my hand, and concentrate. Concentrate hard on your bed, for I sure don't want you landing on that old cement floor!"

                    *   *   *

The transfer took longer this time, and a great deal more effort. Brick decided it was partly because he was so tired, but mainly because he had to build up a lot more power for two people. It sort of worried him to realize how much everyone would soon be depending upon him—for what if his ability failed at the wrong moment? But it was the kind of thing he didn't like to think about, so he tried to put it out of his mind.

They landed safely in their beds, and the first person he saw when he opened his eyes was Nurse Jackson, dozing in the chair in front of him. But the others were awake, waiting and watching.

"They're back!" Lily Rose and Charlie Pill cried together, and Nurse Jackson sat up with a jerk, blinking.

"Heaven be praised!" she breathed. She bounced to her feet, hurriedly rubbing the weariness from her brown eyes, and looked closely at Princess. "Oh, my, that sun did pink you a little," she announced. "Brick caught it, too. I was scared to death you'd get a bad burn—but this shouldn't bother you too much. If it does, I'll put something on it."

"I wasn't out in it long," Princess explained. "I found a shady spot and crawled into it. Oh, I sure hated to come back! But Brick said I should, so I could tell you about it. We've just *got* to go there—it's the most wonderful place! There are strawberries everywhere—wild ones, and they're absolutely the yummiest things you've ever tasted!"

"Strawberries?" Diz Dobie echoed wonderingly.

"Strawberries!" Lily Rose whispered.

"Phooey!" said Charlie Pill. "I don't believe it. Strawberries don't grow wild."

"They did when I was a kid in Alabama," Nurse Jackson told him, and Princess sat up and opened her right hand and said, "Look!"

In her small hand were three slightly crushed but very red and luscious berries. Nurse Jackson passed them around, and they vanished instantly into three eager mouths. While the berries were being relished, three pairs of eyes stared at Princess, who had never been known to sit up before without help.

"You can sit up!" Charlie Pill said in a small voice. Then he burst out, "We've got to go there! And once I get there, I'm not coming back, ever!"

"That's what I want to talk about," Brick said. "I know everybody wants to go—that is, if Nurse Jackson comes with us. You—you told us you'd come," he added, looking at her earnestly.

"I'm not about to stay here," the nurse retorted. "But, Brick, we'll have to plan this carefully, and then move fast. First, I'd better know more about this house you saw. What's it like inside?"

He described it carefully, and told her everything he could remember about it.

She frowned. "Strange. Can't be a residence. Must be a sort of camp, or maybe one of those youth hostels some countries fix up for hikers. Anyway, so long as it's not locked, there can't be any objection to our using it for a while. Did those bunks have any bedding on them?"

"I—I didn't notice."

"Well, it doesn't matter. We'll have to take blankets anyway. Did you have any trouble with those two I gave you?"

He'd forgotten all about them. "I got there with them okay. They must be near the spring where I dropped them."

"I'm glad to know that," she said. "It means you can carry things as well as people, and that's important. Now, let me see. . . . " She sat down and closed her eyes. "You'll need shoes —sneakers if I can get them—jeans, shirts. . . . I think all of us should wear jeans on a trip like this. And socks and towels and handkerchiefs. I can pack everything into laundry bags. And, Brick, you can hang on to a bag every time you take one of us over. . . . "

Suddenly she stopped, and a startled expression came over her broad face. "Why, this is downright crazy! Here I am talking as if we're going on a little camping trip—and we may end up in Australia or on one of the moons of Jupiter."

Princess said, "It can't be Australia, 'cause I didn't notice any kangaroos. But we did see a big black horse and two deer. Oh, they were beautiful!"

Nurse Jackson blinked. "Well, I don't care where it is so long as there are no man-eating beasts and bill collectors." She stood up and began pacing about the ward. "Now, let me see. First, I'd better go down into the basement and see what's in Donations. It'll save time if I can find enough clothing there. If not, I'll have to wait till the stores open in the morning."

Brick was suddenly worried. "If we wait till after daylight to leave, it'll be dark when we get over there. And cold. And that's not all. It—it may take a lot of time to move five of us over there, with our bags and things. And tomorrow they'll be taking the rest of the patients away from Belleview. If any of us are still here . . . " He paused and bit his lip. "You see what I mean?"

"Oh, good heavens!" Nurse Jackson sat down heavily in the nearest chair. "I should have thought of that—but I've been so rushed lately I'm downright addled. Brick, we're going to have to be out of here by daylight—that is, if you can manage it." She jumped up and studied him with sudden concern. "You look beat, son. You've got to have some rest before we can do anything. I'll see if I can whip up something hot to give you a little strength, and while you're resting I'll have a look at Donations."

She hurried away, and returned presently with a tray containing five steaming cups of cocoa and a plate of sandwiches.

"Don't ask me where I stole the milk for the cocoa," she murmured slyly. "Anyway, I thought you all had better have a snack now, and then get what sleep you can. I'll wake you later when the bags are ready."

*   *   *

Cocoa was a rare treat at Belleview, and the others were still sipping theirs, trying to make it last, when Brick finished his and closed his eyes. He was asleep almost instantly.

It seemed that only seconds had passed when he became aware of Nurse Jackson's firm hand on his forehead.

"It's time, Brick," she whispered.

Excitement stirred in him. Then he gasped in dismay as he made out the hands of the clock on the opposite wall. It was

nearly three in the morning. "W-why didn't you call me earlier?"

"Sh-h-h! I don't want to wake the others yet. Brick, I had
trouble. I—"

"What happened?"

"I'll tell you later. We've just got to work fast and do the
best we can. How do you feel?"

There was worry in her. Deep worry. He could sense it in
her and it added to his own rising uneasiness. Whatever had
happened must have been pretty serious, for Nurse Jackson
wasn't one to get upset easily.

"I'm okay," he told her, trying to get confidence into his
voice. "I'm sure I can manage things now."

"Praise be! Everything's ready, and the bags with our things
are right here on the floor. Now, here's the plan: It'll be Diz
Dobie first—I've already switched the beds around so you can
take him ahead of Charlie. Charlie's so weak; I don't want him
to be over there all alone. The girls will follow Charlie, and I'll
go last."

She lifted a laundry bag from the floor and placed it in the
crook of his right arm. Then she went over and quietly wak-
ened Diz Dobie, and tucked a rolled-up blanket under the
brown boy's left arm. "All set!" she whispered.

Brick reached out and firmly grasped the other boy's hand.
"Close your eyes and concentrate on the dandelion place," he
ordered. "And hang on tight!"

This time he deliberately chose the sloping hillside where he
had found himself the first time. Maybe he could have taken
Diz to the second spot, down by the spring, for it would save
steps later when they went to the house; but at this late hour,
with so many trips ahead, he was afraid to risk it. He didn't
even consider trying to reach the house. The first spot was the
place everyone had visualized—in fact, it had turned out to be
exactly the way they'd imagined it—and he was sure by now

that the clearer you could see a destination in your mind, the less time and effort it would take to get there. If you were too tired, you just couldn't reach it at all.

It was a great relief, suddenly, to feel the hot afternoon sun on his face. He opened his eyes and sat up, and saw Diz Dobie staring about in speechless wonder. Hurriedly he moved the bag and blanket they had brought, and had the brown boy crawl well to one side in order to be out of the way when he returned with Charlie Pill.

"I'll land in the same spot," he said. "And Charlie will be where you were. But when I bring Princess and Lily Rose, they'll be on my right. So watch it."

He had no idea what would happen if someone or something chanced to get in his way at the final moment. Maybe it would result in no more than a bad jolting, but he surely wasn't going to risk it if he could help it. After all, you just can't jam two solids into the same space at the same time.

Getting back to Ward Nine, alone and unburdened, was much easier than it had been to leave it. He had barely touched his bed when he heard Nurse Jackson whisper, "Fifteen minutes by the clock. If you can just keep that up, maybe we can make it in time. . . . "

There was no mistaking the urgency in her voice. He had no idea what was troubling her, but he knew every minute must be important. She had Charlie Pill all ready for him, and the next laundry bag was thrust into his arm on the instant. "Get going!" she said tensely.

He did his best to speed it up, but the second trip took much longer than the first. It was a quarter to four when he returned. As he reached for the small hand to his right, Nurse Jackson thrust the third laundry bag upon him. "I've switched the girls," she told him quickly, giving the clock an anxious glance. "I don't want Princess waiting out in that sun till I get there. She's had far too much of it already."

He didn't waste time telling her that the sun had vanished under a great black cloud. He closed his eyes, told Lily Rose to concentrate, and strained to get the two of them away from Belleview.

It was much harder this time. And they were in for a bad shock when they reached the meadow, for they were greeted by thunder and the sudden fierce slash of rain. It was icy, driving rain, and they were immediately soaked. Lily Rose cried out in fright, and he scrambled to help Diz Dobie open up the blankets so the others could huddle together under them.

He was dripping wet and chilled through when he finally landed back in his bed. The hands of the clock showed it was almost five.

"It's storming over there!" he burst out to Nurse Jackson. "You'd better come next and get the gang up to that house. They—they're in an awful spot now!"

"Oh, dear God!" The nurse threw a blanket over him, and cast a stricken look at Princess. "Honey, there's no help for it. I'll have to go. Just be brave, and Brick will be back for you in a little while." Then she caught up one of the bags and took her place on the empty bed to the left.

Brick glanced to the right and saw Princess watching him, lower lip clenched tight between her teeth. Her small pointed face, usually so white, was surprisingly pink from the sun. Her eyes were tragic.

"Don't worry," he whispered. "I'll give it the gun and be back before you know it!"

He clasped Nurse Jackson's strong hand and concentrated on the meadow. The minutes ticked by and he strained and tried to force it, giving it all he had, but nothing happened. Dark fear rose in him.

He could feel the fear in Nurse Jackson now, but when she spoke her voice was calm. "Brick," she said quietly, "you're tired. Rest a while. When you're ready, let me know. Then we'll give it the old double whammy. *That* ought to do it!"

It was with a sudden sinking sensation that he realized what was wrong. Nurse Jackson was a big, strong woman, and probably weighed as much as any three of them. It would take a double whammy, or whatever, to move her.

Brick rested and gathered his forces. It was daylight outside when he finally said, "Let's go!"

This time, with a supreme effort, they went.

And abruptly, with the change, they were in the gloom of storm and pouring rain.

For a moment Brick was too spent to move. Then he made out, on his right, clinging together in a miserable huddle under soaked blankets, the dim forms that were Lily Rose, Charlie, and Diz Dobie. At the sight of them, Nurse Jackson gave a cry of dismay and sprang to her feet.

"Brick, where's that house?"

He sat up and pointed toward the vague line of woods across the meadow. "Over yonder—through those trees. And watch the door!" he called, as she caught Lily Rose up in her arms and began to run. "Don't let it lock on you!"

"Get back to Princess!" she flung to him over her shoulder. "Hurry—before it's too late!"

He still had no idea what was wrong, but the urgency in her voice was plain. He flung aside the dripping blanket that covered him—it was the one she'd thrown over him in the ward, and by some miracle it had clung to him—and closed his eyes against the chilling downpour.

At the moment it seemed impossible to find the energy to return. But the thought of Princess, alone in the ward and in some unimaginable danger, was enough to summon forces he did not know he possessed. It took a while to bring those forces to a working pitch, then abruptly the storm about him faded, and again he was back in Belleview.

He turned instantly to the bed on his right, expecting to see

Princess waiting. Shock held him rigid. Her bed was empty.

It was a frightened and despairing cry of protest, coming from somewhere in the corridor, that jerked him about, trembling. He couldn't make out what she said, but there was no mistaking that high plaintive voice. Someone was taking Princess away.

5

THE LOST BAG

Brick's first impulse, which he obeyed without thinking, was to scramble out of bed and dash for the corridor. He didn't know how he was going to get that far and reach Princess in time, but it had to be done, no matter what happened or what the cost.

His unsteady feet managed to take him as far as Diz Dobie's old bed, then his rubbery legs gave way, and he started to fall. Instinctively he grabbed for the bed, but he was falling in the wrong direction, and his clawing fingers caught only the cotton spread that covered it. He tugged at it wildly, and succeeded only in jerking it free. Yet it broke his fall and saved him from possible injury on the concrete floor.

His rain-soaked pajamas were clinging to him, and he was shaking with cold. While he looked desperately around, hoping to see a wheelchair he could use, he clutched the bedcover about him and then began crawling to the door. He was still yards away from it when he heard Princess cry out again.

Brick scrambled frantically ahead, yelling with all the power of his lungs, "Stop! Stop! Don't take her away! Stop!"

The turn of the corridor was in sight when he heard quick footsteps approaching. Suddenly Miss Preedy, who should have been off duty by now, appeared in the doorway. Behind her loomed a policeman.

"What's going on in here?" she demanded. "Where have you been? What are you doing on the floor?"

"It's Princess—they're taking her away! Please don't let them," he begged. "Please!"

"Shut up!" Miss Preedy snapped. "They're taking her away because I ordered it." Then, in a voice that shook with fury, "Where's that thieving black woman?"

Brick gaped at her. "Nurse Jackson is no thief!"

"She's a thief and worse! I caught her stealing clothes and valuable drugs, and she assaulted me. I've ordered her arrest. Where is she?"

"She—she's gone," Brick faltered, and looked imploringly at the policeman. "Please, won't you help me?"

The policeman ignored Miss Preedy's demand to search the rest of the building. "Is it proper to leave a patient lying on the floor like this?" He stooped quickly, scowling, and said, "What's wrong, young feller?" Then he exclaimed, "Say, your head's wet, and your face is red. Have you got some kind of fever?"

At the word "fever," Miss Preedy turned quickly and stared down at him. Her eyes widened, and she gasped.

Brick bit his tongue so he wouldn't even think of sunburn, which he knew no one would believe anyway, and an electric chain reaction skipped through his mind with a speed and logic that would have shamed any computer.

Abruptly he cried, "Stop Princess! She's got it too! It's contagious—she'll infect everybody! We—we're supposed to be kept here . . . isolated. . . . " He hesitated only a split second while he dredged up the worst thing he could think of, then blurted out, "Dr. Swartz said something about typhus. . . . "

Brick didn't know whether anything as terrible as typhus produced a flushed face or not, but he figured they wouldn't be too well acquainted with it in Belleview either. At any rate, the dread word had the desired effect upon Miss Preedy, for she gave a stifled shriek like a strangling mouse and flew into the corridor.

In a matter of seconds a white-jacketed, white-faced attendant hurriedly thrust a wheelchair containing a tearful pink-faced Princess into the ward, then turned and vanished. The policeman, muttering to himself, took time to lift Brick to a bed, then hastened out, closing and locking the door behind him.

"Oh, Brick!" Princess said in a voice that quavered, "I—I'm so glad to see you I could cry! How did you ever make them bring me back?"

"Tell you later. We've gotta get going. Where's your bag?"

"Right here in the wheelchair. My feet are on it. I told the man it had all my things in it, and that—"

"Can you wheel yourself close to me?" he interrupted. "Hurry!"

But he had hardly spoken when he saw that it was impossible. She was swaddled in blankets, and was securely strapped into the chair. Nor was there space enough between the beds for the wheels to roll, for the policeman had put him on the center bed which had belonged to Charlie Pill. The quickest solution was to get back onto the floor and take off from there.

He slid to the floor and scrambled over beside Princess. She managed to free a hand, and he clasped it quickly.

"Concentrate!" he whispered. "Give it all you've got!"

It didn't help a bit to know that they were bound to be interrupted if he took too long at this. The terrible word he'd uttered would soon be all over Belleview, and then Dr. Swartz would be informed. They had to move fast—but he'd done so much fast moving in the last few hours that he was beginning to feel like a worn-out battery incapable of the slightest spark.

Brick strained. The angry tap of approaching heels in the corridor gave his trembling powers a sudden jolt, and abruptly Belleview faded.

*   *   *

It was such a wonderful relief to see bright stars overhead
that for a while Brick was incapable of movement, nor did he
mind the chill of the rain-soaked grass beneath him. The storm
had passed. Now he could hear only the heightened music of
the brook, and the curious and varied calls of the unknown
creatures of the night.

Then he realized that he still had a tight grip on Princess'
small hand. He glanced toward her. His eyes hadn't yet become
adjusted to the dark, and all he could make out was a vague
blanket-wrapped shape huddled in the wheelchair.

Suddenly he laughed. "Hey, can you beat that! I brought the
wheelchair too! Well, that's one thing we won't need over
here."

"I sure hope not," Princess said earnestly. "Brick, where is
everybody?"

He sat upright, shivering, and peered about while he
clutched a little closer to him the bedcover he had pulled
around him in the ward. Then he made out the sodden blankets a few yards away on the grass.

"Looks like Nurse Jackson has taken them all up to the
house. Don't worry. She'll be back here looking for us in a little
while."

"Oh, I'm not worried. I'm just so happy and thankful to be
here, I—I could sit here for hours and hours! That was absolutely the *awfull*est moment when they were taking me
away. . . ." She gave a little sigh, then asked curiously, "Brick,
what in the *world* did you do to make them bring me back?"

Before he could explain, he heard Nurse Jackson calling
anxiously to him from somewhere in the darkness across the
meadow. He gave an answering cry, and presently he could
make out her dim figure approaching.

"Am I glad you're here!" she told them thankfully. "I've

really been worried. That Miss Preedy almost ruined everything. . . . Now I can't find my flashlight, or even a box of matches. And I'm practically blind in the dark." Then she exclaimed, "Princess! What are you doing in a wheelchair?"

Brick said, "They were taking her away when I got back. Golly, if both of us hadn't been a little sunburned . . ."

"What's sunburn got to do with it?"

He told her about Miss Preedy's coming with a policeman, and how the policeman had mistaken his sunburn for some kind of a fever. "So I just told them it was typhus," he said, "and that Princess had it too. Boy, did they bring her back in a hurry!"

"Typhus!" Nurse Jackson gasped, then roared with laughter. "Typhus! Great day in the morning!"

She stooped and began to fumble with the straps on the wheelchair. "I can't push this thing through the woods," she admitted. "Not in the dark. Princess, you'll have to ride piggyback and be my eyes. Brick, I'll be back for you as soon as I can. We haven't a light of any kind up there, or so much as a match to start a fire, so you can imagine what a crawly mess we're in!"

Though she had spoken as if the whole thing was a lark, Brick realized she was very much concerned. Even with lights, it wasn't going to be any picnic for a while. Everybody except Princess had been soaked in the storm, and all their blankets and bags of clothes were wet—save, of course, the ones he'd brought over last. The chilly night made it a hundred times worse. If they could just manage to get a fire going in that fireplace . . .

While he waited for Nurse Jackson to return, Brick shivered in his thin cover and tried to remember what it was like in that curious building he'd been trapped in. Surely the people who had built it wouldn't have overlooked anything as important as lights. Could there have been a lantern overhead that he hadn't

noticed? Or lamps on the sides, perhaps? Or were the lights
hidden?

He decided they were hidden. In that case, wouldn't the
switch for them be in the usual place, just inside the entrance?

When Nurse Jackson finally carried him to the building—
she had the door carefully propped open with a fallen limb—
he had her set him on his feet just within the doorway. While
he clung to the casing with one hand, he felt over the adjoining
stone wall with the other. But instead of anything resembling
a switch, all his groping fingers encountered was a circular piece
of carved wood. It seemed to be a decoration shaped like a
cogged wheel.

He was examining it, wondering if it had a moving part,
when a small sound beyond the threshold made him turn his
head.

The faint light of the stars made it easier to see outside than
in. Not six feet past the partially open door, the great dark
shape of an animal loomed threateningly.

As he stared at it in a sort of frozen horror, Brick was aware
of all the former occupants of Ward Nine chattering in the
blackness behind him, happy in spite of their misery, and trying
to ignore the chill while they hunted through soaked bags in
the hope of finding something dry to wear. He'd brought them
here, and he couldn't help feeling responsible for them.

Somehow, quickly, that door had to be closed, and there was
only one way to do it. He threw himself forward, reaching for
the broken limb that propped it open. The limb was knocked
aside. It fell in the direction of the dark shape crouched beyond
it, and the thing sprang away and instantly vanished in the
blackness of the trees.

As Brick scrambled back into the room, the big door swung
shut behind him and he heard the outer bolt snap into place.

Nurse Jackson said anxiously, "Brick! What in the world
happened?"

"I—I saw something outside," he told her. "So I closed the door." He didn't add that they were locked in now, and that getting out might be a problem. But at the moment that hardly seemed to matter.

There were sudden uneasy questions from the others. But Princess said, "Oh, I'm sure it was that horse we saw. He wouldn't hurt us. He's just too beautiful."

Brick knew it wasn't the horse, but he said nothing. There was no use frightening everyone by explaining that the thing he saw was more like a great cat, or possibly a wolf. For the first time he began to see a reason for the extraordinarily high fence on the opposite side of the building. He remembered that there was a door in the back wall to the right of the huge window; at night one could go out there without fear of being attacked. Probably the toilets and storage places were located in that area.

Frowning, he pulled himself upright and began groping for the cogged wheel with his fingers. There was a movement in the dark behind him, and Nurse Jackson whispered, "Brick, that was no horse out there, was it?"

"It sure wasn't."

"Could it have been a dog?"

"Maybe. But it was a mighty big one."

"Oh, lordy me! This place is beginning to get me worried. I'd feel a lot better if we had a light."

"I think I've got it."

The cogged wheel, he'd suddenly discovered, turned—but it was to the left instead of to the right. As he moved it slowly, the blackness vanished and a rainbow of soft lights came on around the room. They glowed from a dozen hidden recesses and brightened as he turned the wheel. From the disorder on the floor came gasps of astonishment and delight.

Brick crawled around to the fireplace and crouched before it, studying it thoughtfully. Somehow, they had to have a fire.

He'd never built one in his life, but sticks and chips were already arranged for one here, and all he needed was a match.

Would the people who used this place, who kept everything in such perfect order, have made preparations for a fire and yet left no means of lighting it?

His glance traveled around the hearth, then swept the expanse of stonework rising above it. There was no mantelpiece, but over on the right was a small niche in the masonry. He crawled to it and reached inside. His hand came out with a small slender box made of brass.

The thing opened the long way and disclosed a pencil-like object made of some heavy substance. The interior of the box was lined with a similar material, which was badly scratched.

As Brick puzzled over the pencil, its purpose suddenly became clear. It was a lighter, for when he drew the point of it across the inside of the box, it burst into flame. Even the resinous chips in the fireplace seemed to possess a magic quality, for they flared up the moment he touched the lighter to them. Almost in a matter of seconds the fire that he had kindled became so hot that he was forced to move away from it.

Nurse Jackson, appearing with a load of strange blankets in bright colors, paused suddenly and stared at the fire. "I declare!" she said in an odd voice. "Why, that's fat pine burning —and hunks of resin!"

"What's fat pine?" he asked, eyeing the blankets curiously.

"Pitch pine—pine with the resin in it. We used to burn it down South when I was a kid. And we used to go to a turpentine still and get buckets of resin chips—just like those in the fireplace—to start the wood on a chilly morning. Honestly, I could almost believe—but no, that's impossible." She showed him the blankets. "Brick, look what I found! I can hardly believe it."

"They're really something! Where—"

"That big chest under the window is full of them. And there are mattresses on the bunks, glory be." She paused and glanced at her wristwatch. "H'mm. Almost ten o'clock. That's ten in the morning back at Belleview—but it's after bedtime here. Almost twelve hours difference. It's not easy to get adjusted to a different time, but I'm ready to start right now."

She turned to the others and said, "I've found dry blankets for everybody, so let's turn in. We'll straighten up this mess in the morning."

*   *   *

Brick awoke soon after daylight and stared about him uncertainly, almost in fear. For a moment he hardly knew where he was. He was so accustomed to the sounds of Belleview, with the never-ending grind of traffic in the street, that the present quiet made it seem that all the world had suddenly come to a halt. Then he heard birds singing outside, and at the same time he became aware of a heavenly aroma of cooking that was beyond anything in his experience.

Sitting up, he saw that the fire had been rebuilt in the fireplace, and that the damp clothing had been picked up and arranged over benches to dry. The heavenly aroma came from the alcove to the left of the chimney, where Nurse Jackson was cooking something over a small stove. Everyone else seemed to be asleep.

Brick wrapped his blanket about him and actually managed to walk to the hearth without having to rest. In spite of the uncertainties of their situation, he was so happy for a moment that he felt like singing. Hated Belleview was forever behind them, and they were starting a new life in a strange and wonderful place where everything was different. . . .

Then abruptly came the memory of the unknown creature he had glimpsed beyond the door last night. His spirits sank a little. They sank even more when he saw Nurse Jackson's face. He realized many things must be troubling her, but he hesitated to ask about them.

"That sure smells good!" he began. "What are you cooking?"

"Johnnycakes," she said quietly. "Anything smells good when you're hungry. I found some cornmeal in a jar, and a little cooking oil in a bottle. I had to mix the meal with water, but it's hot food, which we need, and it'll taste fine with molasses. I found some of that in another bottle."

She explained that she had packed sandwiches wrapped in plastic into all the bags, but that these would have to be saved till later, and possibly rationed. "I'll pick some strawberries when I get to it," she went on. "But I'm not about to go out there till I find me a big stick."

She chuckled as she spoke, but it did not hide her uneasiness. "This is the craziest place," she said next. "I just can't figure it. Take this stove. It's electric and it works fine, but I do believe it's handmade. And the bathrooms, if you want to call them that. They're out back—girls to the left, boys to the right. There's running water—but it flows through bamboo pipes. And the wash bowls—they're hollowed out of rock!"

He was staring at her in amazement when she jolted him by saying, "Brick, Charlie Pill was sick all night, and now he's got a high fever. I don't know what in the world to do. I can't find my bag anywhere, and all the medicines are packed in it."

Fright stabbed through him. He swallowed. Charlie wasn't strong anyway, and being caught so long in the cold rain must have been too much.

"Maybe you left the bag outside last night," he suggested. "Everything was in such a jam, what with the storm and all. . . ."

She shook her head. "No, I went out first thing this morning to hunt for it. The blankets and the wheelchair are there, but not the bag. I can't remember what I did with it. We were in such a rush, and Miss Preedy upset me so. . . ."

"What happened?"

"She caught me taking the medicines we needed from the drug locker. I was packing them in my bag. She was going to have me arrested, and there just wasn't time to argue with her. So I tied her up, slapped some adhesive tape across her mouth to keep her from screaming, and locked her in the linen closet. I knew she'd be found soon enough. . . ."

Ordinarily the picture of Miss Preedy bound and gagged would have delighted him, but she had caused too much trouble, and had almost succeeded in breaking up their group. Now Charlie Pill could die. It was all too close for laughter.

He told Nurse Jackson about Miss Preedy and the policeman, then said, "I'll bet anything you left your bag in Ward Nine."

"I won't bet. I'm scared to death you're right."

Brick looked away and swallowed hard. He'd thought Belleview was forever behind him. The last thing he wanted was to go back, but as he thought of Charlie Pill he knew it would have to be done. And the sooner the better.

6

SEARCH

They talked it over quickly. Nurse Jackson didn't want him to go to Belleview again—for some reason she was very uneasy about it—yet she was forced to agree that it was the only thing to do. Everything in the bag was important. Aside from her extra clothes, there were matches, a flashlight, a mending kit, some packages of dried food, a set of kitchen knives, and the priceless medicines.

The others were still asleep when he stretched out on his bunk again and closed his eyes. He'd dressed in sneakers, a pair of jeans, and an old flannel shirt that had come out of Donations, and Nurse Jackson had made him eat two of the johnnycakes for breakfast. They were wonderful with the tangy molasses, and he could have eaten more, but he quickly squelched his appetite when he realized how little food there was for six people.

In spite of being rested, it seemed to take a lot more effort to get away this time, possibly because he hated so much to leave. The last thing he heard was Charlie Pill in the next bunk, for in the past few minutes Charlie had begun to mutter to himself with rising fever. Then abruptly everything faded.

He landed with a crash in the cold dark of Belleview.

Brick was too dazed for a while to comprehend what had happened. Though he remained conscious, it seemed that he

kept sliding away to the edge of blackness, then pain would jerk
him back—pain in his head, in his back, in his elbows. Finally
the blackness receded, and the pain in his head settled down
to a throbbing ache. The rest of him hurt whenever he tried
to move.

Gradually it came to him that he was lying on Ward Nine's
hard cement floor. He hadn't missed his bed, for there were no
beds left in the ward—he could tell that by the vague light that
came through the windows and through the open door to the
corridor. He had, he reasoned finally, arrived at the exact spot
where his bed had been, and from there he'd dropped to the
floor.

Slowly, carefully, he forced himself to sit up. Nothing
seemed to be broken—except possibly his head. That ached
like fury. Then he realized this was no time to be worrying
about his hurts. He had come here to find the lost bag, and he'd
better get it and leave as soon as possible.

The bag wasn't in Ward Nine. Even in the near-dark he
could tell that. Since he'd been here last, twelve or more hours
ago, everything in the ward had been removed except for the
old clock between the windows.

He was almost certain the bag had been left near his bed.
Then the men who had taken everything out must have moved
it. What would they have done with it?

Brick put his hands to his throbbing head and tried to think.
By this time, he remembered, all the patients in Belleview were
supposed to have been carted away to the new hospital. But
would they have hauled off the old beds and equipment at the
same time?

He tried to stand up, failed, then began crawling doggedly
toward the corridor.

At the doorway he stopped and peered worriedly about while
he listened. It was dark to the left, but a light was burning near
the turn on the right where the service rooms and the elevator

were located. The building had the feel of emptiness, but he could hear slow footsteps somewhere in the distance. They seemed to be going away.

Then he caught his breath as he made out the cabinets and the dismantled beds that had been taken from Ward Nine. They were stacked at the turn of the corridor, ready to be carried down in the elevator in the morning. Surely the lost bag would be somewhere near.

In his eagerness he got to his feet and went reeling down the corridor, one hand touching the wall for support. He was almost at the stacked equipment when he lost his balance. He reached out wildly and clutched the nearest thing within reach, which happened to be the head of one of the beds. Several others were leaning against it, and the rollers were still on them. His weight was enough to send them moving out from the wall, and suddenly they fell down with a resounding bang and clatter that seemed loud enough to have been heard all over that part of the city.

Brick fell with them, and was lucky enough to go down on top of the heap without getting his arms caught between the pieces. Even so, he was so badly shaken that for long seconds he could not find the will to move.

He was aroused by a man's voice shouting, "Hey, Mike! What's going on up there?"

The sound of rapid footsteps in the opposite direction jerked Brick to his feet again. He tottered to the nearest door, knowing he had to find a hiding place, and quickly. The door was locked. Desperately he forced himself across the corridor to the only other door within reach. It opened to his touch and he collapsed inside.

He thought his ragged breathing would give him away as someone pounded past in the corridor. With an unsteady hand he fumbled around in the dark, found the safety latch on the door, and turned it. It wouldn't protect him for long if a careful search were made, for the lock could be opened from the outside with a key. If that happened, of course, he could escape by going back to the dandelion place. Only, there was the problem of the lost bag. . . .

Somehow he just couldn't go back without it.

While part of him listened to the men moving about in the corridor, rattling doorknobs and searching, he tried to think of all the possible places where the bag could be.

He hadn't noticed it on the cabinets outside, or on the floor. Then, with a sudden sinking sensation, he remembered Miss Preedy. He felt a little sick. Miss Preedy must have discovered the bag when she returned to Ward Nine after the typhus scare. In that case he'd never see it again.

Footsteps crossed the corridor and paused by his door. A hand turned the knob and shook it. A man said, "I don't think it was a prowler, Joe. It was just those fool beds. They weren't stacked right."

"Could be," came the muttered reply. "But I'd watch it anyway. In this part of town they'll steal the fillings out of your teeth if you sleep with your mouth open."

Brick waited. The men went on. Finally all he could hear was the eternal grind of the surrounding city.

He got up on his knees and felt for the safety latch. Instead, his fingers touched the light switch on the wall to the left of it. He pressed it and discovered he was in a linen closet piled with baskets of odds and ends awaiting removal.

On the floor, within reach of his hand, was a big laundry bag so tightly packed that it was almost beyond his strength to lift it. It took only seconds for his trembling fingers to determine that it was the one he had been searching for.

*   *   *

Brick's relief was so great that for a long happy minute, while he clasped the bag tightly and willed himself back to the dandelion place, his head stopped throbbing, and all his aches vanished.

Then, gradually, as more minutes passed and the expected change did not come, his throbs and aches began again. In rising desperation he tried harder, and harder still, but with the increasing effort his pains increased until he could no longer endure them. He cried out in sudden agony and stopped trying.

Maybe, if he remained perfectly quiet for a while and thought about nothing at all, his head would clear up. But it was no use. His head continued to throb, and the least effort made it worse.

Now in place of desperation came a growing fear. Maybe he had lost his ability entirely. Maybe the fall had cracked his head, and had doomed him to stay in this hated city for the rest of his days. Now he would never know what it was like to live in a place where people didn't use locks on doors, where there was no rumble of traffic, and where you could go out and get all the strawberries you wanted for the picking.

But that wasn't the worst of it. He would never again see those who mattered the most to him—Princess and Nurse Jackson and Diz Dobie, and Lily Rose and poor Charlie Pill. . . .

Tears flooded his eyes. He wiped them angrily. He could take it if he had to—but it didn't seem right that someone like Charlie Pill should die because he, Brick, had received a crack on the head. Anyway, if a guy could do something as crazy and as complicated as teleporting, there was no reason why the same guy couldn't do a simple thing like stopping a headache.

He closed his eyes, told himself that he was going to sleep a while and that when he woke up his head would be healed and everything would be all right.

Brick went to sleep almost instantly. When he awoke, which was very suddenly, there wasn't time to even think about his head, for men were busy in the corridor, and someone was trying angrily to open his door.

In quick alarm he clutched the laundry bag and wished himself back in the dandelion place.

He was there almost in the next breath.

*   *   *

As usual he had brought himself to the familiar spot that he had used so often, and he didn't seem to have an ache in the world. The wheelchair was still where he'd seen it last, but he hardly noticed it. Something seemed wrong.

It took him a few seconds to figure it out, then he realized it was the sun. It was still bright daylight here when it should have been dark. At least, he'd expected it to be dark, for wasn't it morning back at Belleview? Hadn't he slept through the night there, and weren't the men he'd heard just coming to work? He could have been mistaken, but that was the feeling he'd had. And with twelve hours difference in time . . .

Then he forgot the sun's peculiarities as happy cries from across the brook drew him to his feet. Nurse Jackson, evidently out picking strawberries, had just sighted him. Near her, with baskets in their hands, were Lily Rose and Diz Dobie.

Brick tugged the heavy laundry bag into the wheelchair, and pushed it down to the brook and over to the other side. As the others crowded about him, bursting with questions, he asked about Charlie Pill.

"Oh, he's ever so much better," Lily Rose said quickly. "Nurse found some leaves and roots and made a tea—"

"I was desperate," said Nurse Jackson. "When you didn't come back, I knew something had to be done fast. Then I remembered a tea my old granny used to make out of mullein leaves and dogwood root. Brick, I didn't have an idea in the world that I'd find those things growing here, but I did. And in sight of the door! Honestly, this is the strangest place. I could almost believe—" She shook her head. "Anyway, we've been taking turns picking berries and watching for you. Brick, what happened?"

He told them about it while they returned to the building. The sun was getting low, and Nurse Jackson seemed in a hurry to get back. She took over the wheelchair and made Lily Rose, whose legs were failing, ride in it with the laundry bag. As she pressed forward, her uneasy eyes kept studying the shadows. Diz Dobie stumbled silently behind her, unsteady on his feet but helped along by a crutchlike stick that had been fashioned, Brick suspected, mainly as a weapon.

Princess, watching from the door, squealed a greeting to him as they approached, and Nurse Jackson asked, "Did you see anything while we were gone?"

"Seven more deer!" Princess told her, eyes big. "They streaked by so fast I could hardly count them, and went off into the woods yonder." She pointed.

"Did you see what was after them?"

Princess shook her head, and Nurse Jackson said, "Brick, that makes twenty-five deer we've seen today, all of them on the run. Something's chasing them. From now on, I don't think any of us had better leave the place alone, and we should all carry weapons."

For Brick it was a very sobering return. Not that the place lost any of its early magic by the knowledge that unknown dangers were all about them. But it did mean they'd have to be extremely careful until they were strong enough to take care of themselves and knew far more than they did about this baffling and incredible country.

That evening, after a frugal meal of one sandwich apiece and a double handful of plain strawberries, they sat around the fire to talk over the future. Charlie Pill was too weak to be up, but on his insistence they bundled him into the wheelchair and made him comfortable by the hearth.

Somehow, just being able to sit before an open fire made a

doubtful future a lot easier to face. Until they came here, Brick knew, not one of them had ever had that magical experience. And with the wonder of the fire was the great miracle of being able to use bodies again that had long been useless. Of course it would be many days before they all could get about like normal people, but at the moment it was better than a movie to watch the delighted expression on Charlie Pill's face while he toasted his shins and wiggled his skinny white toes. For a long time Charlie had forgotten that he even had toes. Now even the pain he used to have in his frail arms and shoulders seemed to have vanished.

"There's just enough cornmeal left for another batch of johnnycakes," Nurse Jackson was saying. "And we can stretch the sandwiches till tomorrow night. After that, well, there're the beans in my bag, and that dried stuff up there. . . ." She indicated the corn and the onions hanging from the beams overhead.

"What about all the things growing out yonder?" Brick asked, pointing toward the rear window. Beyond it was a small field enclosed by the high fence. With so many deer around, the reason for the fence was suddenly obvious.

Nurse Jackson looked a little sad. "Brick, it's still spring here, or at least early summer. Nothing planted inside the fence will be ripe for a long time. It's all fall stuff that can be stored for the winter—corn, potatoes, pumpkins. . . ." She shook her head. "We're lucky to have strawberries—but they'll be gone in a few days. Then we'll have to look for other things growing wild."

There was a moment of uneasy silence. Then Brick said, "By tomorrow I ought to be able to walk well enough to do a little exploring. It's gotta be done, and I'd sure like to try it. But, well, before I do, I'd feel a lot better if I knew what it is around here that chases the deer." He frowned, then asked, "Would it be wolves?"

"I just don't know," she told him. "It depends on where we are. When I was a kid in Alabama, dogs were the worst. They go wild and run in packs. But I haven't heard them barking."

"How about bears? Do they go after deer?"

"I don't think black bears do. Grizzlies may, but this doesn't look like grizzly country."

"What else would frighten deer?"

"A panther certainly would. There might be one close by."

"A *panther!*" Lily Rose gasped. "Oh, my goodness!"

Princess said, "But a panther is only a cat. I *love* cats."

"Well, I've never heard of a panther actually attacking a person," Nurse Jackson said. "But lots of other animals do. If we could just find out where we are . . . "

"There ought to be some newspapers around," Brick suggested. "That would tell us. Has anybody looked?"

"I've looked," said Princess. "There's not a sign of a paper anywhere on the place. There's not even a book or a magazine. I've looked everywhere except in the upper bunks, and I can't get up there yet."

Nurse Jackson rose, frowning, and made a quick but thorough inspection of the upper bunks. She came back shaking her head.

"That's really queer," she said thoughtfully. "Old newspapers are about the commonest things in the world. Most houses have stacks of them. Of course, this isn't exactly a house. It's more of a camp of some kind, and it seems to be stuck off at the end of nowhere. I'm surprised it has electricity. But no papers! . . . "

"You know what I think?" Princess said in a low voice. "I think we're on a strange planet where they're so unspeakably advanced that they don't bother with the printed word—'specially newspapers."

"Aw, phooey," Charlie Pill muttered. "What's so advanced about not having papers?"

"Because, silly, advanced people know they're not worth reading. If they were, they'd be read for years. But who ever looks at yesterday's paper? So, if you were truly advanced, you wouldn't even bother with them. You'd use telepathy."

"Huh? *Telepathy?*" said Charlie Pill, and Lily Rose exclaimed, "Of course! They'd do like we did in Belleview. They'd tune in. Maybe we ought to try tuning in here."

"I've been trying it," Diz Dobie told them. "But all I get is music, and it's so far away I can't tell anything about it."

"What about people?" Brick asked. "Can you pick up any of their thoughts?"

The brown boy shook his head. "I can't get a thing like that. We—we must be an awful long way from anywhere."

In the following silence Brick watched a stick burn through in the fireplace and slowly dissolve into glowing red embers. *An awful long way from anywhere* . . . An unknown place full of unknown dangers—and because he'd brought them all here, it would be his fault entirely if they starved to death or got killed by savage beasts.

He swallowed, then squared his shoulders. Well, they weren't starving yet, and he wasn't about to let them—not as long as there were deer outside, and he could figure a way to kill one. He didn't like the idea of killing anything, but he'd sure do it if it had to be done.

Right now, the important thing was to find out where they were. There ought to be some way to do it.

He glanced at Nurse Jackson. "You don't believe we're on another planet, do you?"

She chuckled softly. "At this point, Brick, I'm ready to believe anything. I'm like the person who didn't believe in flying saucers—till he saw one. As for being on another planet . . . " She paused, then said, "We could be. Certainly anything is possible. But when I got up this morning and opened that big door yonder—"

"How—how'd you open it?" he interrupted. "I couldn't budge it when it locked me in here."

"Why, I just pushed the knob, or whatever it is in the middle of that carving, and it opened right away. But if you couldn't stand up and put your weight on it—"

"That was the trouble," he admitted. "So I tried to turn it. But what about this morning?"

"Well, when I opened the door and went out," she continued, "it really gave me a shock. I took one look at those pines and I said, 'Great day in the morning! I'm right back in Alabama where I was born!' Brick, if I didn't know better, I'd say we were up in the hill country, not fifty miles from Birmingham."

"Honest?"

"I mean it! Everything's the same—the pines with the resin cups on them, the color of the clay, those clear springs out there, the dandelions and the wild strawberries, and even the very rock they used in this building. I just can't get over it."

"Then—then maybe we *are* in Alabama."

She shook her head. "I don't see how. With twelve hours difference in time? And summer instead of winter? Or almost summer, though I don't quite understand these cool nights."

"Could we be in Australia?" he asked. "Or New Zealand?"

"With resin cups on the pines? Certainly not."

"What's a resin cup? I mean, I saw those things on the trees, but—"

"A resin cup is anything you hang under a slash on a pine tree to catch the resin that drips down. From resin comes turpentine. That means there must be a turpentine still somewhere near. Maybe, if we can find it . . ."

She rubbed her eyes wearily, and he saw her glance at her wristwatch. She gasped. "Why, I didn't know it was *that* late! We should have been in our bunks two hours ago. Or has my watch gained time?" Then she shook her head. "No, it's never acted up before. It has to be right. To bed, everybody!"

As Brick wheeled Charlie Pill to his bunk, he suddenly remembered how he'd returned here to daylight when he'd expected to find it dark. Something seemed to click in the back of his mind, and for a moment he almost saw an answer.

But before he could get a tight mental grip upon it, the thought slid away like quicksilver. Even so, he was able to catch a fragment of the truth.

Time had something to do with where they were. Maybe, if he could figure it out, it would explain everything.

Time.

7

WHERE ARE WE?

Brick found it almost impossible to get to sleep that night. For one thing, he'd slept too long in the linen closet at Belleview, and he wasn't a bit tired. And, like many a transocean plane traveler who has flown from daylight into darkness, he was not yet adjusted to the change. So for long he lay awake, wondering about that twelve-hour difference between where they had been and where they were now. In fact, it seemed to be a little over twelve hours, depending on how you figured it.

Finally a curious thought, like a strange bug, came flitting through his mind and suddenly bit him. The result of this biting was a stream of equally curious thoughts that left him breathless.

Suppose, he reasoned, that it actually took just as much time to teleport to a certain place as it did to travel there by more ordinary means? Only, instead of traveling all those hours and being aware of them, you sort of sidestepped them and got there ahead of time? Wouldn't that explain it all?

Well, not quite—unless it worked in reverse when you went back to where you started from. *That* would do it. For wasn't it perfectly logical that those hours you'd sidestepped would catch up with you when you went in the opposite direction?

It was a beautiful theory, and he couldn't see a flaw in it until he remembered the difference in seasons.

That sort of boggled him for a while. Then it occurred to him that if you can sidestep a few hours, why couldn't you just as easily slip around a few weeks or a few months? It made sense. Well, it made sense enough if you stretched things a little. Even Einstein had had to stretch things once in a while.

He was wondering what Nurse Jackson would think of his theory when the earth outside seemed to shake to the pounding of heavy feet, and the big door shook as a huge body brushed against it. This was followed almost instantly by a shrill outburst from many throats, a wild madness of sound as if all the fiends of darkness were in pursuit of the monsters that had just gone by.

Brick huddled in his bunk, overcome with a dread such as he had never known before. Those horrible sounds couldn't have been made by earth creatures. They came from *things*, the unknown inhabitants of a strange planet. He had no doubts about it now. They had left old Earth far behind and had gone to another star system. The people who had built this place probably weren't people at all. More likely they were ghastly humanoids of the kind he had read about—green-spotted blood drinkers who would hang them by their feet and drain them for a feast.

In his fear he started to call out to Nurse Jackson, then he heard her slow steady snores across the room, coming from the bunk between Princess and Lily Rose. It seemed incredible that the terrible racket hadn't awakened her, but everyone appeared to be sound asleep. He was suddenly thankful that the big door swung outward instead of inward, or one of the monsters might have forced it open. Outside now it was quiet, and the only sounds were those familiar peepings and tick-tockings that he was beginning to find rather pleasant.

Brick decided it wouldn't help to wake up anyone now and

get them all alarmed. It would be bad enough when they learned the awful truth in the morning.

He worried himself to sleep finally, and when he awoke it was bright daylight. Everyone was up and dressed and practicing how to walk on their unsteady legs except for Charlie Pill, who again had been placed in the wheelchair. Nurse Jackson had exchanged her rumpled white uniform for what appeared to be a pair of workman's coveralls, which had been in the lost bag he'd finally brought back from Belleview.

"I got them in Donations with the rest of our clothes," she told him. "They're just the thing to wear exploring. Eat your cakes and we'll get started—that is, if you feel up to a little walk. The others are going to wheel Charlie down to the meadow and pick some berries and things for supper. I think it's perfectly safe today."

He swallowed, and burst out, "No—no! It's not safe! I'm sure now we're on a strange planet." Then he told them what he'd heard during the night.

Only Princess seemed undaunted by the prospect of being lost on an unknown world full of frightful beasts. She clapped her hands and exclaimed, "Oh, this is utterly breathtaking! If I can just get to *see* those things! . . ."

"Well, I've an idea what one of them was," Nurse Jackson muttered. "Or rather, what two of them were—because there were two of the big animals. Let's go outside, Brick. I want to show you something."

He followed her out, and the others crowded to the door, wheeling Charlie Pill with them. Just beyond the flagstones at the entrance she stooped and pointed. There on a stretch of bare ground were some easily recognizable prints.

"Horses made those," she said. "I saw them when I came out earlier. They're grazing down there by the stream. One's black—I suppose he's the same fellow you told me about—and they're huge. To anyone who's never been around horses, or heard them go stomping past in the night, they'd sound like a pair of dinosaurs. As for those other things that made so much racket—"

She looked around, and shook her head. "I just don't know. Possibly they were birds. Anyway, I don't think they were dangerous. I don't believe there's any danger near us this morning."

"Why do you say that?" he asked.

She pointed toward the meadow. "See?"

Beyond the trees he could make out the winding stream. A herd of deer were grazing peacefully beside it. Near them were the horses—the great black one he'd seen before, and a beautiful pale one with a white mane. "If there was anything to worry about," she told him, "they'd show it. When we go out, we'll all keep an eye on the animals. The moment they act frightened, we'll hurry back here."

*   *   *

When they set out upon their exploratory trip after breakfast, Brick carried only a small adze-like tool he had found in the shed out back. He could cut or dig with it, and its handle was long enough to make it a good weapon in an emergency. Nurse Jackson had located a stout basket in which she had placed two sandwiches for their lunch, and one of the knives that had been in her lost bag.

They left the others picking berries and dandelion greens near the spring, and began to follow a trail that skirted the fence and took them westward along the edge of the meadow. The horses raised their heads and watched them as they went by, but the deer paid little attention to them except to move shyly aside when the trail swung too close.

"Those deer are practically tame," Nurse Jackson said curiously. "Why, I don't believe they've ever been shot at. So it can't be a hunting camp we're staying in. Anyhow, there are no guns in the place."

"There's a crossbow hanging on the wall inside my bunk," Brick told her.

"A *crossbow?* Well, I never!"

He'd been so tired the first time he saw the thing that he hadn't paid much attention to it. Then he'd forgotten it entirely, for there were all sorts of odd tools and objects and stringed instruments hanging about the walls and in the bunks, and he'd supposed they'd been put there for decoration. But now he wasn't so sure. His bunk was the one nearest the door, and it was just possible that the crossbow was kept there for protection.

Or were there other crossbows in the place, and were they used as silent hunting weapons? He hadn't yet had time to look carefully at everything, nor had he even considered taking the crossbow with him this morning. It seemed far too difficult to use. He felt safer with the adze.

The high fence was hardly out of sight behind them when Nurse Jackson stopped abruptly and pointed. Ahead, at the edge of the pines, was a small shed with a round ovenlike affair beneath it made of stone. It was topped by a copper dome. A stone chimney led up through the thatched roof. Piled on one side were a number of plastic kegs.

"What is it?" he asked.

"It's the turpentine still I've been looking for," she told him.

His wobbly legs were already giving out as he went stumbling on behind her, and he was glad of the chance to collapse under the shed while she moved about, shaking her head and muttering to herself.

"What's wrong?" he asked.

"Everything and nothing," she said. "Brick, I was raised in turpentine country, but I never saw a still as small as this. Why, it wouldn't pay a body to run it. On top of that it's pretty. With that thatched roof, it's downright picturesque." She shook her head again. "Who ever heard of a picturesque turpentine still, especially one with thatch on the roof?"

"But why shouldn't it have a thatched roof? That place where we're staying has one."

She sighed. "Brick, you just can't have thatch around a turpentine still. It catches fire too easily. I don't know why this place hasn't burned down years ago, but I'll bet it's been here for ages. I don't understand it."

"Maybe it's not real thatch," he said.

The idea seemed to startle her. The roof was low, and by standing on her tiptoes she was able to reach up and grasp a few pieces of the overhanging straw. They refused to break, and she was forced at last to get her knife and cut off a piece.

"What d'you know!" she exclaimed. "It's not straw after all. It's imitation thatch—plastic!"

The roof, she found, was covered with bundles of little plastic tubes. The tubes seemed to be filled with a powdery substance.

"Well!" Nurse Jackson said at last. "I think I've figured it out. We're on a millionaire's estate. He wanted everything to be picturesque, with thatched roofs and all, but he used plastic thatch so it would be safe."

It seemed to Brick that the plastic tubes had another purpose more important than just being pretty, but at the moment he couldn't think what it was.

"If this is on an estate," he said, "why isn't there a road so you can drive here in a car?"

"Oh, the owner of a place like this would probably come by helicopter. He could land anywhere around on the meadow."

Brick felt doubtful. "I wouldn't think a millionaire would want to bother with anything like a turpentine still. And why isn't there a lock on that big door back there? I mean, that

place has been there a long time, and a lot of things in it must
be valuable. Why haven't they been stolen?"

"That sort of bugged me too," Nurse Jackson admitted.
"Take those blankets I found in the chest. All handwoven, the
finest things I've ever seen. If they were mine, I'd sure keep
'em under lock and key. But there they are. Anybody can walk
right in and walk right out with 'em. So I figure we're in the
middle of a huge estate, thousands of acres, maybe, with a steel
fence all around it and guards to watch over it." She hesitated,
then added, "The only thing I *can't* figure is the difference in
time and in season—that is, if we're in the South, like I think
we are."

"You still believe we're in Alabama?"

"Well, it could be Mississippi, Georgia, or somewhere in the
Carolinas or Virginia." Suddenly she pointed. "See that tree
yonder? That's a sassafras. I know, because when I was a little
girl I used to dig the roots of one of those trees so we could
make tea. Brick, the *only* place you'll find a sassafras tree is in
America. It's the same with those big pines behind us. They're
what we call yellow pines, and the only place they grow is in
the South. You see? So we're bound to be in one of the states
I mentioned. But why is the time different?"

"It could be because we teleported here," he said, and began
explaining the theory that had come to him during the night.
But somehow, as he told it in the bright light of day, the theory
didn't sound so hot. Nurse Jackson listened to it politely, but
seemed far from convinced. "Anyhow," he finished lamely,
"I'm sure time has something to do with it."

She chuckled. "Of course it has. That's what's really got us
bugged." She glanced at her wristwatch, gasped, then studied
the sun and looked at her watch again. "Speaking of time, my
watch is acting crazy. The sun tells me it's only about ten in
the morning, but the watch says it's past noon. It's gained all

of two hours since we've been here. Do you s'pose teleporting did that to it?"

"It must have. Look what it did to us!"

His eye was suddenly attracted by a carved wooden disc on a post. He went over and turned it, and was rewarded by a bright glow of light from the rafters above.

As he stared at it, Nurse Jackson said, "That's funny. There's no power line coming in here. But maybe there's an underground one leading from the bunkhouse."

"That must be it," he agreed, as he turned off the light. "Say, that gives me an idea. If we can't find a road anywhere, then all we have to do is to follow the power line that comes into the place, and it'll lead us to people."

She nodded slowly. "And we may have to locate some people soon, Brick. It all depends on how much food we can find. It takes an awful lot when there are six mouths to feed. That dried stuff won't last long, and we can't live off dandelion greens. Some of you need meat—especially Princess and Charlie Pill."

"Maybe I can kill a deer with the crossbow."

She looked at him sharply. "I doubt if Princess would eat it if you did. But we'll see. If we don't locate a road in the next day or two, I think we'd better plan to follow the power line and see where it goes."

*   *   *

Before moving on, she borrowed his adze and dug some of the roots of the sassafras tree and put them in her basket. Later, near some monstrous oaks at the lower end of the meadow, she found a curious brown mushroom, pitted and crinkled, that started them upon an eager search that lasted into the afternoon. His legs had nearly given out now, and to save them for the walk back to the bunkhouse he did his searching on hands and knees. The pitted mushroom, he learned, was a morel. It appeared only in the spring, and they were lucky to find a spot where so many of them had been overlooked by the deer.

"We used to call 'em hickory chickens when I was a kid," Nurse Jackson told him happily. "Best eating things on earth! Better than beefsteak. Don't pass up any—they'll be gone tomorrow, and there won't be any more till next year."

Her basket was nearly full of mushrooms and roots when he glanced back up the meadow and saw the deer moving swiftly away. She noticed them at the same time, and caught up the basket with one hand and pulled him to his feet with the other. They started back the way they had come, her hand on his elbow to steady him.

They did not speak until they had passed the turpentine still and could see the upper part of the meadow and the tall fence on one side of the field. Charlie Pill and the others had evidently returned to the house, for the only living things in sight were the two great horses. They were pawing at the ground and tossing their long manes while they watched something in the woods on the opposite slope.

"W-what d'you s'pose they're afraid of?" he whispered.

"I don't believe they're afraid. They act more upset and angry. Those are wild horses, Brick, and I've an idea they'd fight the thing if it would come out. I think it's a panther. I've been watching for tracks, and I saw some smudged ones that made me think it's some kind of a cat. They were too big for a dog."

They had reached the corner of the fence now, and abruptly his uncertain legs crumpled under him again. But now he saw something he had not noticed before. It was a gate. It opened outward just as the big door in the building did, and when they were safely on the other side it swung shut and automatically bolted itself. He realized suddenly that both door and gate had been planned to swing as they did so that animals could never accidentally open them, even though they were not locked against humans.

"Are panthers spotted?" he asked, as they started slowly along the edge of the field.

"Why, I've never heard of such a thing. What made you ask?"

"Well, it sort of seemed that the animal I saw the other night was spotted. I'm not sure. Maybe it was just the way he looked to me in the starlight. And he was big."

"Oh, lordy me! Don't tell me we've got a leopard or a jaguar to worry about!"

"I hope not, but I think we'd better learn how to use that crossbow. Now let's find the power line and see which way it runs."

They looked carefully all around the building. There was no sign of a power line anywhere. Nor, for that matter, was there any sort of apparatus that remotely resembled a generator for creating electricity, or a system of batteries for storing it. Yet there was all the power they needed to run the stove and keep the place blazing with light.

Did it just come to them out of the air?

*   *   *

Their meal that night consisted of dandelion greens, fried mushrooms, sassafras tea, and heaping dishes of wild strawberries. No one minded the lack of salt and pepper on the greens and mushrooms, for Nurse Jackson had found enough things growing in an herb garden out by the fence to give them a hint of seasoning. Everyone was hungry, and they could have eaten more, but half the food had to be saved for tomorrow.

Afterward, a small fire was kindled in the fireplace—it was more for cheer than for heat, for the night had turned warm —and they all sat about it to talk over the puzzles of the day.

Brick listened but said little. He was tired and he wanted to go to bed, but his mind was churning with questions. The answer to everything, he felt, was somewhere in this room. It was just a matter of looking for it in the right spot.

Ignoring his aching legs, he got up finally and began moving slowly about the place, peering at the objects hanging on the walls and within the bunks. He discovered a second crossbow hanging on the back of the end bunk used by Diz Dobie. The short arrows in the woven quiver looked deadly, and obviously were not intended for target practice. His eyes swung to the tools—the chisels and other things whose use he could not even guess—and went on to the musical instruments. There were some that looked like flutes, and others with strings that were strange to him. As he studied them, he realized they had two things in common with all the other objects in the room. They'd been produced by highly skilled craftsmen, and they'd been made to be used.

He could hear Nurse Jackson repeating her belief that this was part of a millionaire's estate, but suddenly he knew she was wrong. The people who used this place came only twice a year —in the spring to plant the field out back, and in the fall to harvest it. How they got here or where they came from, he couldn't guess; and far from being millionaires, he had a feeling they didn't even use money. In fact, he couldn't see a thing here that might have been bought with it. Even the dishes and utensils had a handmade look.

So, in spite of the trees Nurse Jackson had pointed out, this couldn't be in America, where money was so important. Where in America were people so smart they could draw power from the air, and so honest they didn't use locks to keep strangers from entering?

As Brick closed his eyes, he could almost see the people who came here. They loved to make things, and song and music poured out of them; they didn't seem at all like the kind whose lives were bound up in newspapers. But wouldn't they have books? Surely they would!

Then where were they?

His glance went swiftly around the room, and suddenly fastened on the big chest where the colorful blankets were stored. He went over and raised the top, and held his breath while he dug down under the remaining blankets.

The books were there. The entire bottom seemed to be covered with them. He hauled one out and opened it, and stared blankly at the strange page of type. It was printed in an unknown language. Even the letters were unfamiliar.

Frowning, he reached down again for another book. Instead, his hand touched what seemed to be a heavy roll of paper. He drew it out and slowly unrolled it. It took a minute or more of careful study before comprehension came.

Suddenly he turned and shouted, "Hey! Look what I found!"

8

EXPEDITION

He brought the long piece of paper he had un-
rolled over to the table and tried to spread it out. It would not
lie flat until he had placed the book at the upper edge and a
pair of earthenware mugs at the lower corners. The others
crowded around, and Nurse Jackson lifted Charlie Pill from the
wheelchair so he could have a better view of it.

"Why, it's a crazy map of some kind," Charlie Pill muttered.

"There's nothing crazy about it," he told Charlie. "It's just
in a language you don't understand. Latin or Greek, maybe."

"It's not Latin," Nurse Jackson said. "No, and it's not Greek
either. I don't recognize those characters. But I do know it's
an original drawing by a very fine artist. It's a beautiful piece
of work."

Princess said breathlessly, "It's absolutely unspeakably gorgeous!"

"Sure is," Diz Dobie agreed, and Lily Rose said, "If only we
could read it!"

"We don't have to," Brick told them. "It's a map of this part
of the country. See, here we are right down here!"

The map was about two feet wide and more than twice as
long, and it was drawn in exquisite detail and tinted with
watercolors. Birds, animals, and flowers decorated the open
spaces, along with symbols placed near tiny squares indicating

buildings. His pointing finger touched a square at the bottom. "This is the house," he said. "And here's the field. And there are the two springs coming together to make the stream. Yonder's the turpentine still."

A stringed instrument drawn beside the square for the house showed that it was a place where people came for fun as well as for work. An ear of corn and a pumpkin decorated the field, and a pinecone gave the clue to the still. Two horses had been drawn grazing in the middle of the meadow.

Princess squealed when she saw them. "They are the same horses that are out there now!" she exclaimed. "They must be pets."

Brick was more interested in tracing the course of the stream. After much winding, it went all the way to the top of the map, where it entered what seemed to be a river. Here were grouped many squares indicating houses, showing that a community of some size existed by the water. No straight lines for roads were on the map, but there were many winding dotted lines that he decided must stand for trails.

Excitement stirred in him as he studied the community at the top of the map. He pointed to it, and looked at Nurse Jackson. "How far away d'you s'pose that is?"

She shook her head. "Brick, there's a distance scale in the corner, but unless we knew what it meant it would be hard to guess. If it's a quarter of a mile to the turpentine still, then it must be at least sixty miles to the town, or whatever it is. Probably more, because the trail winds with the stream."

Sixty miles. Could they ever manage to walk that far? They couldn't do it now, of course, but maybe in a week or so they'd be able to tackle short distances and camp out each night. With an unknown animal on the loose, the idea of camping out didn't exactly appeal to him, but they couldn't stay here all summer waiting for somebody to discover them. Not with the strawberries giving out, and nothing but dandelion greens to eat when the dried stuff was gone.

What had they better do?

He was studying the map again, his eye attracted by a bit of blue indicating a lake, when he heard Nurse Jackson say, "I give up. This can't be a millionaire's estate. Why, there must be a thousand square miles of wild country shown here. And there's not a single road in it, and only one tiny little town. I'd feel better if I could hear just one plane go by. . . ."

Lily Rose said, "Maybe they don't have planes here. Maybe, like Princess said, we really *are* on another planet."

"Phooey!" said Charlie Pill. "How could we be on another planet with the same trees and animals and everything? That's crazy."

"No, it isn't," Princess told him quickly. "Haven't you ever heard of a *sister* planet, a sort of *invisible twin*?"

Diz Dobie said, "I have. It would be just like Earth, almost, only it would be in another dimension."

"Hey, maybe you've got something," Charlie Pill admitted. "Maybe, coming here the way we did, we sort of jumped from one dimension to another. What d'ya think, Brick?"

"Maybe that's it," Brick said. "It sure would explain a lot of things."

He didn't tell them he was beginning to get another idea. Only, it was such a dinger, and it sounded so crackpot, he decided he'd better keep it to himself until he'd dug up a little proof. Turning to the blanket chest, he hauled out a half dozen books and opened them upon the table. Everyone exclaimed over them because they were so beautifully bound and printed, but they were in the same language as the map—Nurse Jackson had never seen anything like it—so he learned nothing from them. Pictures might have told him a lot, but the few illustrations were of botanical subjects and no persons were shown.

He had turned back to the map when Nurse Jackson glanced at her watch, then shook her head and said, "I don't know what time it is, gang, but it sure feels late to me. Let's call it a day."

Tired as he was, the map held him. Finally Nurse Jackson came and peered over his shoulder.

"What is it, Brick?"

He pointed to the small lake that had caught his attention earlier. "Wouldn't you say that's about fifteen miles away?"

"Something like that. But I'd allow for twenty."

His finger touched a fish-shaped symbol beside a tiny square indicating a building. "And wouldn't you say that's a sort of camp like this one? A place where you can catch fish?"

She bent closer over the map. "Why, I believe you're right! I didn't notice that before."

His finger moved upward, following the course of the main trail and the stream. Scattered throughout the area, some on the stream and others on side trails, were more tiny squares with symbols beside them. A few of the symbols were obvious, but he guessed that others stood for raw materials or ores. It was easy to see how the people in the village lived. When they needed something, they set out on one of the trails and got it. With comfortable camps like this one in which to stay, probably whole families went along and had fun while they worked.

He touched the house with the fish symbol again, and looked at Nurse Jackson. "W-what d'you think?"

"I'm thinking the same thing you are," she said quietly. "If fish can be caught there, that's where we ought to be right now."

"Then let's plan to go. When we get there, we can rest a while and catch lots of fish, then keep on going till we find people."

"Brick, could you teleport us there?"

He shook his head. "Not unless I knew exactly what it looks like—which I don't. I'd be crazy to try it. We—we'll just have to hoof it."

"But, Brick, we can't go anywhere till Charlie Pill can walk a little better. And Princess isn't strong enough. . . ."

"They'll be better in a few days. We can't wait too long."

She sighed. "We sure can't. We'll talk it over with everybody in the morning."

*   *   *

' After a scanty breakfast of strawberries, tea, and some of the remaining mushrooms, they held a conference. Surprisingly, in spite of the fact that they might have to spend several uncertain nights camping out in the forest, everyone was eager for the trip except for Lily Rose. The golden-skinned girl thought they ought to remain where they were.

"But why?" Brick asked.

She shook her small dark head. "I—I don't know why. It's just how I feel."

Suddenly Princess said, "If Lily Rose feels we ought to stay here, then we should. Don't you know that you can always trust feelings better that thoughts?"

Charlie Pill said, "Aw, phooey!" and Brick said a little grimly, "I don't want to go against anybody's feelings, but if we stay where we are now, we'll have to start killing the deer so we can eat."

"Oh, no!" Princess cried. "I'd rather starve!" And Lily Rose added almost tearfully, "It would be awful to kill wild things. Especially here."

"I don't see why," Brick said. "People do it all the time in hunting season."

"B-but not *here*," Lily Rose persisted. "It—it would be all wrong. Don't you *feel* it?"

Brick did feel a little uncertain about hunting in this new land, but he said only, "Okay, just so long as you don't mind eating fish. When we get to the other camp, we may have to live on fish entirely for a while."

Once the decision was made to leave, they went immediately

to work. It took them four days to get ready, but when they left at dawn on the fifth morning they had enough extra food to last them at least until the third evening. The dried corn they had found hanging from the beams was their mainstay. It had been shelled and converted into meal in a hand grinder discovered in the shed, then mixed with some of the onions and baked into cakes. When the cakes were gone, they would have the remaining onions to fall back on, plus a small plastic bag of rice that had been among the things Nurse Jackson had packed in her bag at Belleview.

As they started slowly down the trail past the fence, Brick glanced back with sudden regret at the comfortable bunkhouse. He wished they didn't have to leave it, but there seemed to be no other solution. They'd cleaned the place carefully and put the fine blankets back in the chest, and even laid fresh materials for a fire in the fireplace. The only articles they'd borrowed, which he hoped to return later, were necessities like spoons and some kitchenware, and the two crossbows.

They didn't dare travel without the weapons. When they made camp tonight, they would sleep under the Belleview blankets, and he and Diz Dobie and Nurse Jackson would take turns staying awake and doing guard duty. The three of them had spent part of an afternoon with the crossbows, learning how to handle them.

Brick felt his first twinge of uneasiness as they filed past the turpentine still. While he examined the meadow, dim in the dawn mist, he paused a moment to shift the new shoulder strap holding his laundry bag, then again he gripped his crossbow with both hands so he could carry it in a ready position. The weapon was cocked and loaded, the short arrow being held in place by a clip that would automatically release it when he pressed the trigger. It operated like a gun, and he knew it was just as dangerous, so he was careful to keep it pointed to the left and toward the ground. Because he was steadier on his feet than Diz Dobie, who walked ahead, he had been given the rear position, for there was less chance of his stumbling and accidentally discharging an arrow.

Up ahead Nurse Jackson, who was pushing the loaded wheelchair—it had been turned into a cart to carry their extra gear —stopped to give Charlie Pill a chance to rest. In the past few days the thin boy had learned to use his legs better, but he was forced to walk with a stick and he was much too weak to carry a bag.

As Brick studied the meadow, not liking the emptiness of it, he was suddenly aware that the sky was turning red. Remembering his first incredible sunrise, he called to the others to watch. This second one was just as awesome, and Nurse Jackson was so moved by it that she murmured in astonishment, "Great day in the morning! I'd forgotten the Lord made sights like this!"

When the great burning disc was above the trees, she said to Princess, "There's something different about it. You could be right. Maybe we really are on Earth's twin." She shook her head. "Well, let's get moving, gang. We've got some ground to cover before dark."

Only now did Brick see the horses in the rising mist. They were standing rigid with flaring nostrils, staring at something in the shadows on the opposite slope. He could make out nothing, but he had the uncomfortable feeling that he was being watched.

The feeling stayed with him as he trudged on after the others. A coldness began to knot in his stomach.

*   *   *

The coldness was still in him at midday when they stopped to rest and to eat a single corn cake apiece. He had lost count of the number of rest periods they had been forced to take.

"How far do you think we've come?" he asked Nurse Jackson.

"Possibly a mile and a half," she said quietly.

He chewed worriedly on his lip. At this rate it would take them a week to get to the fish camp.

She said, "Just pray the weather holds, and we'll be all right. If we run out of food, I'm sure we can find enough wild stuff to do us." She studied the sun a moment, which seemed to be at zenith, then carefully set her watch by it. "Maybe it'll work this time," she added hopefully.

"When you check it tomorrow," he said, "I bet it'll be an hour fast."

"But, Brick, what's wrong? Is it only the watch?"

"Dunno for sure yet. I'm just sort of guessing."

He still didn't have anything to prove the idea that had come to him, and it sounded much too crazy to talk about. Nor did he mention his belief that they were being followed. He hadn't been able to sight the creature, and he was beginning to believe they had nothing to fear from it till dark.

As they tramped onward, much too slowly for his peace of mind, his dread of the coming night was somewhat offset by the excitement he felt at every new turn of the trail. He knew the others shared his feeling, but Nurse Jackson's growing wonder surprised him.

"Look at those oaks!" she exclaimed once. "The *size* of them! Why, it's like a great park here."

It was, indeed, very parklike in places, and he could see long vistas under the spreading limbs, often with deer shying away from them. Birds and squirrels were everywhere.

"Wasn't it like this in Alabama?" he asked.

"Maybe once," she said. "But not in my day. Brick, this is all virgin country. It's never seen an ax."

"Have you noticed any strange trees, or queer birds or things?"

"No, they're all familiar. But I do think it's peculiar that we haven't seen a rabbit yet. Or even a snake. I just can't understand it."

Brick thought he knew the answer to that, but he said nothing.

The trail was fairly open and hard underfoot, and seldom did Nurse Jackson have much trouble with the wheelchair. The worst spot was at a rocky ledge, just before they stopped for the night. Here all the gear had to be unloaded and carried down separately. By the time this was done, they were glad to make camp and gather wood for a fire.

With the ledge at their backs and a fire in front of them, Brick felt they were safe. Even so, he slept fitfully on the hard ground after his watch was over, and every small strange noise brought him up on his elbow, listening.

The night seemed endless. But nothing happened, and in spite of muscles that were beginning to ache with every movement, he was glad to be up at dawn and help Nurse Jackson begin the ordeal of the second day.

This new section of the trail seemed only a repetition of the part they had covered already. The only noticeable differences were the rockier ground and the widening stream. By noon the rocks were making the wheelchair difficult to handle. Brick unloaded it, and with Diz Dobie to help he managed to remove the small swivel wheels at the back. Now the chair could be tilted and drawn easily like a cart.

Just before they continued their journey, he remembered Nurse Jackson's watch. As he had predicted, it was an hour fast.

She looked at him worriedly. "Brick, I'm beginning to believe you know something I don't. What is it?"

He shook his head. "I'm still guessing. Did you happen to see the moon last night?"

"No. It was too misty. Why?"

"Oh, nothing much. I haven't seen it many times in my life, and I'd sort of like to know what you thought of it."

Princess said, "Wouldn't it be just too utterly breathtaking if the moon here turned out to be a sumptuous pink? I simply adore pink." Then she added, "Brick, do you know how to catch fish?"

"Well, I've read about it. All you have to do is to bait a hook and drop it into the water."

"Does it hurt the fish?"

Charlie Pill said, "Aw, phooey! Don't you know fish haven't got feelings?"

"I certainly hope not," she said uneasily. "But it's upsetting to think they might have. We're going to be awfully, awfully hungry when we reach the lake—and I just love fish. But I don't believe I could bear to eat one if it came screaming out of the water. I'd simply rather starve."

Brick had already made up his mind that, before he allowed any starving to be done, he would secretly kill a deer and bring in the meat without telling what it was. But before he could do that he realized he would have to destroy the creature that had been following them. Its presence frightened the deer, so that he almost never saw them except at a distance, running. He'd given up wondering why the thing continued to shadow them. So far it had stayed well out of sight, but he could still feel its presence, and several times by watching carefully he'd caught the vague movement of it through the trees at their rear. He was sure by now that it was spotted.

The thought of the thing was chilling enough, but of equal concern was the knowledge that their food was going to run out long before they reached the lake. Charlie Pill seemed to realize it too, for the thin boy did his best to walk faster. He kept it up till they camped that night, and he managed to hold a steady pace all through the third morning. But at noon he collapsed.

"Why don't the rest of you guys go on ahead and start catching fish?" he pleaded. "That's the smart thing to do. I'll follow soon's I can. You can have a ton of fish all cooked and ready to eat by the time I get there."

"Nothing doing," Brick told him. "We're sticking together. It's not safe to be alone."

Nurse Jackson agreed with him, and before going on, she made Charlie rest for two hours while they searched the immediate area for wild greens and mushrooms. When they made camp that evening she cooked the rice that she had been saving, then added the wild things to make it go farther.

By careful rationing, the rice lasted until the evening of the fifth day. Brick was hungry when he rolled in his blanket that night, but they'd all been hungry for several days, and a few more hours of it didn't seem to matter. The fish camp, surely, couldn't be more than a mile or two away, and they were bound to reach it some time in the morning.

A sudden slash of rain drove them up at dawn. They packed hurriedly and took to the trail without bothering to make tea.

"We'll have a real breakfast in a little while," Nurse Jackson promised confidently. "We're almost there, and there's bound to be plenty of cornmeal and stuff for cooking fish. And, gang," she added, "keep those blankets over your heads. I don't want anybody catching pneumonia. There'll probably be a stack of dry blankets at the camp."

In spite of hunger that was beginning to gnaw, and thin overworked muscles that ached so badly that it took courage to keep wobbly legs moving, they turned it into a game and laughed at the rain and made up silly songs and chanted them as they trudged along. Noon came, and still there was no sign of the new camp. They huddled for a while under a tree, resting, then set out again, slower now and chanting only occasionally. By midafternoon they were silent.

But somehow they stumbled on, urged by Nurse Jackson, who kept repeating with a cheerfulness Brick knew she couldn't feel, "Just a little farther, gang. We're almost there."

Then Charlie Pill began to chant feebly, *"We're almost there. . . . We're almost there. . . . "* How Charlie Pill did it and kept going, Brick didn't know, but he added his voice to Charlie's, and soon everyone was chanting, *"We're almost there! We're almost there!"*

And suddenly they were there.

First there was a shout from Diz Dobie ahead. Then he cried, "I see the fence! And there's the thatched roof!"

But when they came through the dripping trees and stood beside him, no one could say anything.

There was the fence, and they could see the roof at the corner of it. But there was no house, and no lake. The thatched roof covered only an open shed no larger than the turpentine still. In front of it, where a lake had been, there was only a broad empty area of sand and mud, with the shallow stream winding through the middle of it. The stream flowed down through a recently washed-out break in an ancient earthen dam covered with trees.

Brick felt as if the end of the world had come.

9

SINGING IN THE SKY

If anyone spoke a word while they dragged themselves up to the gate and entered the place, Brick was not aware of it. The shelter was almost a duplicate of the one over the turpentine still, except that it had a fireplace on one side instead of the ovenlike apparatus for heating resin. A picnic table and a few benches occupied the center of a stone floor. The tall fence surrounding a small apple orchard enclosed two sides of the structure, but hardly gave a feeling of security against the unknown dangers of the night.

As for food, it was obvious that none had been left here. Some fishing poles for catching it lay across the beams overhead, and various utensils for cooking and eating it filled a low cupboard to the left of the chimney, but that was all. Brick could hear water running from what seemed to be a spring out back, but he was too tired to investigate it. What they needed now was a fire.

He removed the arrow from his crossbow, then tossed it and his soaked blanket on the table and crouched by the fireplace. The last visitors here had left wood and kindling arranged inside, ready for the lighter, and in less than a minute he had a roaring blaze going. As it sent out its drying warmth, everyone huddled before it. At the moment, they were too miserable for speech, and too exhausted and disappointed for further thought or action. They wanted only to rest.

Brick glanced at Lily Rose, who had known all along that they shouldn't have left the bunkhouse. "Thanks for not saying 'I told you so!' " he mumbled. "Golly, I sure goofed when I got the idea for coming here. We should have stayed where we were."

Her peaked face broke into a sudden smile. "Oh, this isn't so bad," she managed to say. "It's ever so much better than Belleview, and—and anyhow, look what we did! If we can come this far, we can go the rest of the way."

Nurse Jackson hugged her. "That's the spirit, honey. And we'll make out. Don't any of you ever think we won't. I've been sitting here trying to remember something about a plant I saw out there where the lake used to be. It's just now come back to me. Brick, Diz, let's go out yonder and dig for our supper."

She took the adze and a basket from the gear on the converted wheelchair, and led them through the gate and over into the soft ground where the lake had been. Here grew hundreds of long-stemmed plants with leaves like huge arrowheads. When they tugged on the now-wilted leaves and dug down with the adze, they found large tubers that resembled potatoes.

"Duck potatoes!" Nurse Jackson said happily. "We'll really feast tonight!"

And feast they did. Maybe it was because he was so hungry, but those duck potatoes, boiled over the fire and with no seasoning but their natural sweetness, seemed to Brick the best things he'd ever tasted. The others enjoyed them just as much, and Charlie Pill said, "Boy o' boy, I'd walk twenty miles for a taste of these!"

"You just did," Nurse Jackson chuckled. Everyone laughed, and she added, "Believe me, gang, that's a real miracle. When I think how crippled all of you were two weeks ago . . ."

It was almost dark now. Brick piled more wood on the fire to help dry out their blankets, then looked speculatively at a wooden disc on one of the posts. It was just like the disc at the turpentine still. He went over and turned it, and was rewarded by a flood of soft light from above.

Nurse Jackson blinked at it and shook her head. "Will you tell me how they get power 'way out here at the end of nowhere, without a line or anything?"

Brick nodded wearily. "I think it's the thatch. It—it soaks up power from the sun and stores it in those straws."

"But, Brick, that seems almost too advanced—"

"Not for these people."

"These people," said Princess, "are absolutely unspeakably advanced, and I can prove it. Real early this morning, before the rain got us up, I—I saw something. . . . I—I didn't tell you about it because it was so—so utterly shattering and breathtaking that . . . that I wanted to think about it first. . . . " Her pale head was nodding, and it was becoming hard for her to speak. She managed to add, "But I'll have to . . . tell you about it in the morning. . . . Right now I'm . . . just . . . too . . . tired. . . . " Her head fell forward, and she was suddenly sound asleep.

Brick was so exhausted himself that he had little recollection afterward of curling up in a barely dry blanket, for consciousness ceased the moment his head touched the floor. After five nights in the outdoors on the hard ground, the smooth stone surface felt almost comfortable.

Something awoke him abruptly at dawn.

For a minute or two after he opened his eyes he lay still, listening, wondering what could have disturbed him. The fire in the fireplace had gone out, and a red glow was spreading from the eastern horizon. In the west a giant moon was setting. The color shocked him, for it was actually more pink than gold. He was aware of the soft splash of water from the spring, and an assortment of peepings and tick-tockings—mainly crickets and frogs, he knew now—mingled with the sleepy twitterings of birds that were only half awake. But none of these had disturbed him. He'd heard something else. What could it have been?

All at once it came to him. He'd heard singing.

Brick sat up. *Singing?* Yes, and it had come from overhead.

He flipped his blanket aside and moved quickly in his bare feet to the edge of the shelter and glanced up. There was nothing in the rapidly reddening sky but a lone bird flapping over the empty lake, and the great pink moon riding the darkness in the other direction. He could see it better now, and he studied it curiously. A few nights ago he had briefly glimpsed it in the mist, but he hadn't been able to tell much about it. Singing in the sky—and a pink moon. Princess ought to love that.

While he changed from his dry pajamas to his not-so-dry clothing, he began to wonder if the singing had actually been overhead, or if he'd merely heard it in his mind. Maybe he'd been tuning in while he slept, and had not realized it. But no, he'd heard it with his ears—and it had come from the sky.

Frowning, he got kindling from the pile of wood behind the chimney and started a fire in the fireplace. Still puzzling over the riddle, he went out to get water from the spring, but he'd hardly taken three steps from the shelter when there was a sudden movement beyond the fence, and pandemonium broke loose. It was like that night back at the bunkhouse when all the fiends of darkness had begun to shriek together. Only here it was worse, for the fiends were closer, and there were no walls to muffle the sound of them.

Abruptly everyone in the shelter was awake and calling out in alarm. Brick glimpsed a flock of birds as big as chickens fanning out into the weed-grown orchard at his rear, but his attention went to the creature beyond the fence that had frightened them.

Before he could get a clear view of it, Nurse Jackson had

appeared beside him, her sturdy form draped in a blanket. "Guineas!" she burst out happily. "Real live guineas! Didn't dream they were here—but that means we'll have eggs for breakfast." She sighed. "They do make a horrid racket, don't they? Such wild things, and they seem to have gone wild here. Papa used to raise 'em when I was a kid, and I should have realized they were what you heard that night. . . . Brick, what are you staring at?"

He pointed silently through the fence. She turned and gasped. The thing that had frightened the birds was standing in the open not a hundred feet away, a dead guinea clenched in its mouth. By comparison, the big bird seemed no larger than a quail. The thing was the spotted creature that had followed them here, and it was huge.

She shook her head. "Oh, lordy," she breathed. "That—that looks like a dog—but it *can't* be. It's too big!"

"It's the thing I saw outside the door that night," he whispered. "It followed us here."

"Followed us?" she said, aghast. "Why in heaven's name didn't you tell me?"

He shrugged. "You had enough to worry about. And—and I didn't want to scare the others. What kind of dog has spots like that?"

"A Great Dane. That's what it looks like—only it has to be the biggest great Dane on earth!"

At that moment Princess rushed over, whispering, "What is it? What is it?" Then, when she saw it, "Oh! What an utterly wonderful, beautiful dog! I wonder if he'd let me pet him?"

"Don't you dare go outside that gate!" Nurse Jackson ordered. "Great day in the morning, I'd as soon pet a tiger!"

The monster had been standing motionless, staring back at them. Now it turned abruptly and bounded away into the trees.

For the first time Princess glanced in the other direction and saw the moon. It was just touching the treetops, and it seemed larger and more pink than ever. He expected Princess to clap her hands and to squeal in delight at the sight of it, but she didn't. It was Nurse Jackson who squealed, and it was a sound of astonishment and awe. Princess said quietly, "I *thought* it was pink when I saw it yesterday morning, then the mist covered it, and I wasn't sure. I—I've got something to tell everybody—but maybe I'd better wait till after breakfast. It's just too utterly, utterly—there's simply no word for it—to face on an empty stomach. 'Specially at this hour."

*　　*　　*

When they finally sat down at the picnic table, it was to the most satisfying breakfast they'd had since leaving Belleview. Not only did their search through the overgrown orchard produce all the guinea eggs they could eat that day, but a panful of ripe raspberries as well. If the eggs were plain boiled and without seasoning, no one seemed to mind it in the least, nor did they mind plain raspberries with nothing on them. At the moment everything was wonderful.

Now Princess said dreamily, "Early yesterday morning I woke up suddenly, and—and you'd never believe what I heard!"

"Was it singing in 'the sky?" said Brick.

Her mouth hung open. "H-how did you know?"

"I'm only guessing," he told her. "Go on."

"Well, that's just what I heard! And it was so absolutely unspeakably lovely that I decided I must have died before my time of hardship and starvation, and that the angels were coming down to get me. Then I opened my eyes and *saw* them!"

"You—you *saw* them?" he blurted.

"Of course I saw them! They were in a gorgeously beautiful boat, and they were coming down from the moon—that great big sumptuously pink moon that all of you saw this morning. . . ."

Charlie Pill said, "Phooey! You're just making this up."

"I'm not making it up! I did too hear singing in the sky, and I did too see the boat with the singers on board, and it went by right over my head."

Brick said, "What happened next?"

"Nothing happened. They just went on, and that's when I realized they weren't angels and that they weren't coming for me after all. They didn't see us because we were lying in the shadow, but I could see them, at least the ones on the right side. They were all young people, just like us, and they went drifting by in that beautiful boat, drifting and singing. . . ."

Charlie Pill said, "Are you sure it wasn't a glass gondola, like the one we used to travel about in on the Martian canals?"

Princess beat her small white fists on the table. "Charlie Pill, you're utterly unspeakable! I'm not making this up, and I didn't imagine it. I heard the singing, and I saw the boat—"

Brick said, "What was the boat like?"

"Oh, it was long and slender, like a sailboat without sails— a beautiful sailboat with fins, and it gleamed. I had the feeling it could go like the wind, but it was just drifting when I saw it. And I saw it for only a few seconds. First I heard the singing, then I opened my eyes and saw this beautiful gleaming boat with the moon behind it, all misty and pink. The boat drifted past, and it was gone in the mist before I could get a good look at it. I couldn't tell much about the singers, except that they were all young like us. After that, it started to rain."

"Did the boat make any sound at all?" Brick asked. "I mean, as if it had a motor or something."

"All I could hear was the singing."

"They must have been pink moon people," said Charlie Pill. "And I'll bet they had a silent motor that ran on moonbeams. What d'ya think, Brick?"

"I'm pretty sure they were real people."

"In a boat?" said Charlie Pill. "In the *sky?* Running on *moonbeams?*"

"Why not? I mean, just being in a boat in the sky, drifting along, proves that they must have antigravity. Which means—"

"Which means," Princess put in quickly, "that the people here must be absolutely unspeakably advanced, just as I said earlier. And if they want to run their boats on pink moonbeams, I'll just bet they could do it!"

"Aw," said Charlie, shaking his head. "This is getting crazier and crazier. Why would a bunch of kids be up at four o'clock in the morning, singing anywhere, let alone in the sky? Where would they be going?"

Brick said, "I don't know, but I've got some ideas about it. If the moon was behind them when Princess first saw them, that means they were going east. This morning early, when *I* heard them singing, they were going west—"

"*You* heard them?" Charlie Pill gasped.

"I sure did. That's what woke me up. But I was too slow, and I missed seeing the boat. Anyway, when Princess saw them, I'll just bet they were heading for the bunkhouse on some sort of holiday, and that they went back home this morning. . . ."

"*Singing . . .*" Nurse Jackson whispered.

"A boat in the sky . . ." Diz Dobie muttered. "This really is crazy."

"And a pink moon," Lily Rose said wonderingly. "This can't be Earth. . . ."

"But the main thing's the boat," said Nurse Jackson, looking a little sick. "We missed it. If we'd just stayed where we were—"

"Maybe the boat didn't stop there after all," Brick suggested. "Maybe—"

"Maybe nothing. It stopped there. That's one of the reasons

the place was built. I can see that now." She shook her head. "If I'd just had the sense to make us stay there—and I would have if I'd only known about the guineas. Why, we had it made there! Now I can remember seeing duck potatoes and wild asparagus growing all along the stream—but I'd forgotten what they were. It's been so long since I lived in the country. . . ."

"Aw," said Brick. "Don't blame yourself. Coming here was my idea. Anyhow, we sure don't have to stay here. We can go back to the bunkhouse, or we can take a chance and go on."

Suddenly everyone was silent. If the bunkhouse had been only a few hours away, Brick knew, there'd be no question about turning back. But the bunkhouse lay nearly a week's weary journey behind them. Maybe it wasn't so far in actual miles, but it had taken all they had to get here. As for going on . . .

A little chill crept over him as he remembered the map he'd found, and realized how much farther it must be to the town. At the rate their undeveloped muscles were forced to travel, it might take them more than a month to cover the distance. And what if they got there and found it wasn't a town after all? He'd just supposed it was because of the little squares indicating houses. But they could just as easily stand for shelters like this one. The place might be no more than a large picnic area.

Nurse Jackson was saying, "One thing's certain. No sky boat, or whatever it is, is going to stop here. This is just a shelter for hikers. And I can see now why there are no roads or cars. These people don't need 'em. Not with antigravity."

She sighed and stood up. "Well, gang, we shouldn't try to decide anything now. We need a couple days to rest up and find some groceries. Brick, I'm going out to dig some more duck potatoes. Feel like giving me a hand?"

He followed her to the gate. She thrust it open and stopped short, and he heard her sharp intake of breath. Then he saw the great spotted dog standing where the edge of the lake had been, only a few yards away.

No one had noticed it appear, and it was a shock to see it again. There was something terrible in the way the monster stood motionless, watching them. Suddenly it gave a low growl of warning, as if defying them to take another step forward.

Nurse Jackson backed quickly and closed the gate. Brick's mind was made up in a flash, and he whirled to the shelter and caught up his crossbow. Hurriedly replacing the arrow he had taken from it, he turned to the fence and took aim between the high palings.

Before he could pull the trigger, both Princess and Lily Rose were beside him, begging him to stop. "You mustn't!" Princess cried. "It would be awful if you hurt it. It's not going to hurt us."

"You're both crazy," he muttered. "Try going out that gate, and see what happens to you."

Reluctantly he put the weapon aside, though he doubted the ability of both Diz Dobie and himself to do more than wound the creature. That, he realized, would probably make it more dangerous than ever.

No one went out of the gate that day, and the great dog did not leave.

10

THE SINGERS

Long after the others had gone to sleep that night, Brick lay awake thinking. Even if the great dog meant them no harm, their situation was serious enough. Such wonders as duck potatoes and guinea eggs were only where you found them, and they wouldn't last forever. Nor were there too many raspberries left, and Nurse Jackson had said it would be months before the apples in the orchard were ripe.

But food was only part of it. There was Charlie Pill's weakness. How Charlie, and even Princess for that matter, had managed to tough it out until today, he couldn't understand. This was no place for them in a storm. What would happen if they ran out of food, and got caught in a weeklong spell of bad weather?

As he remembered the comfortable bunkhouse, he suddenly wished with all his heart that they could be back there, wrapped in those wonderful soft blankets instead of here on a hard floor in the flimsy coverings from Belleview.

Well, why not?

He'd almost forgotten what he could do, and he was so startled by this solution to their problem that he sat bolt upright, wondering why he hadn't thought of it before. If he'd brought them all the way from Belleview to this curious land —and he was only now beginning to guess the immensity of the distance—it shouldn't be any trick to teleport them back to the bunkhouse. The switch would solve everything for a while. And it would get them away from that terrible dog.

Brick was on the point of waking everyone and carrying out his idea immediately. Then he remembered his last experience in Ward Nine, when he'd knocked himself for a loop by aiming for a bed that wasn't there. It would be a lot smarter to wait till morning and fix up a foolproof spot where he could take off and return, so no one would get hurt.

Finally he lay back and tried to sleep. But sleep would not come, and his thoughts kept wandering to the bunkhouse. He could see the interior of the place perfectly in his mind, and he was suddenly a little startled by the realization that it had contained neither a radio nor a television set. Why?

Of course, he could sort of understand about the lack of television. He hadn't even missed it since being here, and he had a pretty good idea by now that the people here were much too interested and busy living and doing the things that mattered to be bothered with manufactured amusements. But radio?

Then he remembered their futile search for a newspaper. And Princess had said that if you were truly advanced, you wouldn't bother with such things. You'd use telepathy.

Telepathy! Did they really use it here? He and the others had tried tuning in several times, but all they'd ever picked up was music. Very faint and distant music. Not once had they managed to tune in on any thoughts floating around.

But maybe that wasn't the way it was done. Maybe you had to send out a definite thought to a particular person before you could expect an answer. It would be a little like trying to telephone someone. Only, you couldn't reach anyone on the phone without knowing his number, any more than you could teleport to a certain spot without knowing exactly what it looked like.

Brick puzzled over this a moment. Suddenly it struck him that he was very much like a castaway at sea, and that all he could do was to send out a distress message and hope that somebody would pick it up.

"Hello!" he began experimentally. Though his lips moved without sound, he put all the force of his mind into it. "Hello! Can anyone hear me?"

He waited a moment, then called again, "Hello! If you can hear me, please answer. We need help!"

He was wondering how much a difference in languages would matter when suddenly, and so unexpectedly that it came like an electric shock, he was answered. The voice that spoke into his mind was as distinct as if he were actually hearing the sound of it.

"Hello! Your call is heard. This is Sender replying. Who are you? Where are you?"

*   *   *

This direct and surprisingly clear communication was beyond anything in Brick's experience, and he had hardly believed it possible. Back in Ward Nine they'd learned to pick up each other's thoughts and feelings to a certain extent, but never like this. Before he could pull his startled wits together, Sender spoke again.

"This is Sender. I answered your call. Did you hear me?"

"I—I heard you," Brick managed to say at last. "You sort of surprised me. I—I didn't know people could really talk this way. Your voice is so clear!"

"It should be clear. I am the strongest communicator on this continent. But you surprise me. You have amazing strength yourself. You nearly took the top of my head off! Who are you? Why haven't I heard from you before?"

Brick was a little shaken. He toned down his mental force

a bit. "Is—is this better?"

"Much better! Now tell me about yourself."

"My name is Brick. There are six of us, and we teleported here from Belleview. That's a hospital—"

"Hold it! You say you teleported here?"

"Yes. I—I had to make a lot of trips to get everyone over. I'm not very old, and I could bring only one at a time."

"You are young? A boy? And you brought all the others? This is amazing. No wonder you can communicate with such power. All of us who can communicate well can teleport for short distances—but we do not yet have the ability to carry another person. Where did you say you are from?"

"We—we're from Belleview. That's a city hospital. We were cripples. We—"

"Hold it. You must realize that we speak different languages. When we send thoughts to each other, they activate the right words for those thoughts in the other's mind. So you must be careful to visualize your thoughts, especially in the matter of names for places and things. You say you are from a hospital, in a city? Visualize that hospital. Visualize the city and the people. We do not have cities here, so I know you are from afar. So tell me again about yourself, and visualize the planet and the shapes of the continents, and the location of the city. Then I will know exactly where you are from."

Brick did so. He could feel Sender's growing shock as he brought to life in his mind the planet Earth, with the only part of it he had ever known—the spreading vastness of noise and ugliness and decay that was the city, with its pressing millions on their eternal grind to live.

"Enough!" Sender said abruptly, as the vision of the city was followed by one of Belleview and its miserable inmates. *"No wonder you wanted to leave! Now let me show you where you have arrived."*

The quick pictures that came to Brick left him gasping.

"Do you begin to understand what you have done?" Sender
went on.

"Yes," Brick said weakly.

*"You have made an incalculable journey. It has never been
done before. Everyone here will want to meet you. You will
understand better when you know that our last city fell to dust
more than a thousand years ago."*

Brick could only gasp.

"We do not miss it," Sender added. *"Our planet is a garden
again. Today all men help their neighbors, and no one profits
from another. But more of that later. Our task now is to find you.
Can you tell me where you are?"*

Brick immediately ran into difficulties. Though it was soon
established, by the fact of darkness, the moon's height and
certain star patterns, that they were on the same continent, it
was evident that a great distance separated them. Nor did it
help much to give a careful description of the bunkhouse and
their present surroundings.

"The land is broad," Sender reminded him, *"and there are
countless trails and shelters for hikers. What we need is a
distinguishing landmark. Do you remember seeing a line of
mountains, or a tall hill?"*

"No," said Brick. "Nothing like that." Then he thought of
the beautifully drawn map in the blanket chest that had been
the cause of their leaving the bunkhouse. He tried to visualize
it for Sender, but it was impossible to remember the ornate
wording, done with strange characters in an unknown language. Without names, the map was useless.

"Keep trying," Sender urged. *"All we need is a clue. If you
can think of one before midnight, I will tell the dawn singers
and they will surely find you in the morning."*

"Dawn singers?" Brick was instantly curious. "Who are
they?"

Sender seemed surprised. *"You have never sung to the dawn?"*

"What for? Why, I—I never saw a sunrise till I came here!"

Now Sender was shocked again. *"This is incredible! But I forget where you are from. And perhaps in the city no dawn was worth rising to, so they went unsung. Here it is a magical time. The world is reborn and song pours from every throat. But the most magical time of all is when the moon is fulling. Then the dawn singers gather in their craft and float singing through the sky. . . ."*

Sender was silent a moment, then he said, *"I will alert the singers anyway, so they will be on the watch for you. But if we only had some idea of the area you are in . . . Perhaps, if you could tell me of the kinds of trees growing around you . . ."*

Save for pines, Brick hardly knew one tree from another. But Nurse Jackson knew. "Wait till I wake the others," he said. "Maybe I can find out something."

He quietly awoke Nurse Jackson, but he had hardly begun to explain about Sender when the others awoke also. They crowded about, listening with growing excitement.

Nurse Jackson could think of nothing that would help. "All I can say is that it still looks like part of Alabama—though it could just as easily be the Carolinas or Virginia. But that wouldn't mean anything to him. I know now we're on another planet. Look at that big pink moon!"

"It's just impossibly gorgeous!" Lily Rose said softly, moving to the edge of the shelter for a better view of it. "It makes you want to go drifting away under it, singing and singing—"

Her voice died abruptly. She went rigid, and Brick saw that she was staring, not at the moon, but at the gate.

The gate was slowly, quietly, being opened by something huge on the outside.

*   *   *

The moment, and the sudden shattering fear that went with it, was something that Brick knew would be forever engraved on his memory. In the bright moonlight his unbelieving eyes could make out the monstrous shape on the other side of the palings. It was the great spotted dog, and the creature had lifted the latch with its mouth and stepped back to open the gate. Now, as Brick stood frozen, staring at it, the monster gave a little jerk of its mighty head that sent the heavy gate flying wide. Then it entered.

In the back of his mind Brick was only partially aware of Sender calling urgently, *"What is it? What is wrong?"* But there was no time to pull his wits together and answer. He sprang for his crossbow, but even as he snatched it up he realized it was empty, nor could he see the arrows anywhere within reach. He dropped the useless thing and grabbed the adze by the fireplace.

"What is the trouble?" Sender called sharply. *"Is anyone in danger?"*

"Yes!" he said, hardly realizing he was speaking as he whirled to face the intruder. "It's that—that monster! That spotted dog! He followed us here—he's just now opened the gate and come in. I—I've got to stop him somehow."

He sprang forward, adze raised. But Princess was quicker. She sped past him, past the motionless Lily Rose who seemed powerless to move, then slowed and began speaking softly as she approached the spotted beast with her small white arms outstretched.

Sender was calling, *"No! Do not hurt the great dog! He is your friend! That is Janico. He is the warden of the South Preserve."*

Brick dropped the adze, which he knew would have been all but useless against such an adversary. The sudden relief that flooded over him left him weak and trembling. He saw Princess with her arms around the great dog's neck, and he said thankfully to Sender, "I wouldn't have believed it! But it's okay now. He's found a friend."

"*Good!*" Sender replied. "*He's highly intelligent, but very shy. Janico is known everywhere. His strain was developed to guard the deer and the other rare animals from extinction by the big cats. He is the only one of his kind left on the continent, so now we know you are somewhere in the South Preserve. But it is a very large area—*"

"Are there horses in the preserve?" Brick asked abruptly, and sent a mental picture of the horses he had seen.

"*Just those two!*" came the surprised reply. "*You saw them?*"

"Yes. In the meadow near the bunkhouse."

"*That is where they are usually seen. Then you must be in the first shelter west of there! I will tell the singers immediately. If some are close, they may find you before dawn . . .*"

They were much too excited to sleep after that. They built up the fire in the fireplace, then sat watching the sky and listening, their excitement mounting as the fulling moon swung westward.

Nurse Jackson whispered, "Brick, you know something I don't. It has to do with time. My watch—"

"It'll always be fast," he said. "The days are longer than they used to be. And the moon is closer."

"Brick, what are you trying to tell me? Why—why is this so much like Alabama?"

Even though he had guessed the truth, the fact of it still boggled him. "It's because this—used to *be* Alabama. But that was ages ago. Ages and ages ago. I—I don't know how it happened, but when we came here, we—we came into the future."

The huge Janico, lying beside Princess, suddenly raised his great head. Lily Rose said breathlessly, "I hear them!"

Now Brick could hear them, faintly in the distance. He sprang up with the rest as the first boat drifted across the moon. Others followed, circling downward. The voices that came from them were the happy voices of the young, and they sang in welcome.

Janico thrust open the gate. Brick and the rest moved through it, slowly, wonderingly, yesterday's children going to meet the children of tomorrow.